Jean
Ethel mrs
midge

Harlequin, the world's No. 1 best-selling publisher of romance fiction, is proud of its tradition of bringing to women everywhere its beautiful and appealing love stories...

 Harlequin Romances—warm and wholesome novels that take you to exciting faraway places and reveal the delights of true love.

 Harlequin Presents—sophisticated and modern love stories that offer the thrill of exotic locales, and the passions and conflicts of love.

 Superromance—longer, exciting, sensual and dramatic new novels, truly contemporary stories in keeping with today's life-styles.

D0596485

What readers say about Harlequin romance fiction...

"Harlequin books are the doorway to pleasure."
E.W. Hawthorne. California

"They are quality books—down-to-earth reading! Don't ever quit!"
G.F. Buffalo. Minnesota

"A pleasant escape from the pressures of this world."
C.T. Hickory. North Carolina

"Keep them coming! They are still the best books."
R.W. Jersey City. New Jersey

One Hot Summer

by

NORREY FORD

Harlequin Books

TORONTO • LONDON • LOS ANGELES • AMSTERDAM
SYDNEY • HAMBURG • PARIS • STOCKHOLM • ATHENS • TOKYO

Original hardcover edition published in 1974
by Mills & Boon Limited

ISBN 0-373-01818-5

Harlequin edition published October 1974

Second printing October 1977
Third printing March 1980
Fourth printing June 1981

Copyright © 1974 by Norrey Ford.
Philippine copyright 1980. Australian copyright 1980.
All rights reserved. Except for use in any review, the reproduction or utilization
of this work in whole or in part in any form by any electronic, mechanical or
other means, now known or hereafter invented, including xerography,
photocopying and recording, or in any information storage or retrieval system,
is forbidden without the permission of the publisher, Harlequin Enterprises
Limited, 225 Duncan Mill Road, Don Mills, Ontario, Canada M3B 3K9. All the
characters in this book have no existence outside the imagination of the
author and have no relation whatsoever to anyone bearing the same name
or names. They are not even distantly inspired by any individual known
or unknown to the author, and all the incidents are pure invention.

The Harlequin trademark, consisting of the words HARLEQUIN ROMANCE
and the portrayal of a Harlequin, is registered in the United States Patent
Office and in the Canada Trade Marks Office.

Printed in U.S.A.

CHAPTER I

Jan Lynton had already discovered Rome was at its most attractive in the early mornings, before the tourist coaches and their loads began perambulating through the narrow streets and fascinating piazzas which opened one out of the other like a box of tricks. She didn't in the least mind being the first in the hotel dining-room, or pushing her way into the single-decker trams and buses which were so cheap and crowded.

The handsome boys, slim as dancers, dark hair curling into slender necks, dark eyes flashing with amusement, disappeared into offices and shops. The girls, wide across the eyes, pointed chins plump and soft, vanished too, when the buses disgorged. Jan had seen those faces so often, in paintings and statues, this last week, that it seemed natural to see them in flesh and blood.

Then, for a little while, there was just Jan; flower-sellers setting up their stalls; the orange-sellers, the sellers of hand-made jewellery and leather goods; the artists, arranging their watercolours to catch a buyer's eye.

This way, she felt part of the Roman world; as much at home as she was in London. She felt sorry for the tourists, goggling out of their air-conditioned buses like goldfish in bowls.

She had not intended to come to Rome alone. It had been Jan-and-Michael for so long. Mike was a history student, crazy to see the Forum, Pompeii, a dozen other places dating back over two thousand years. Then, without reason, the bottom fell out of their relationship. Quite suddenly, it was Jan alone.

Today she wanted to see the Spanish Steps again. Funny how the guide books and postcards showed the

Steps empty and covered with azaleas; never as they really were, swarming with the international young wearing the international uniform of faded blue jeans and skinny tops. Some had things to sell, paintings, flowers, jewellery. Some were hippy types, bearded and dirty. Pale-haired Scandinavian girls, clean as new wood. If one sat long enough, and watched, half Shakespeare's characters walked up and down the Steps. Romeo and Juliet, hands clasping, heads bent together, oblivious of the world around them. Dark Othello.

The Steps were empty now. But as Jan began the long climb up to the top, to the twin towers of the church of Santa Trinita dei Monti, her eye was caught by the figure of a man walking down. Slim, tall, well-dressed in an elegant suit of light blue-grey; a marked contrast to the usual crowd haunting the place. Now who was he? Her eyes wrinkled, concentrating on the Shakespeare game. One of the Two Gentlemen of Verona, obviously. Valentine—that was the one.

Suddenly he seemed to catch sight of someone he knew. Hesitated, as if to make sure; then came running lightly down the Steps at such a speed that Jan crossed her fingers for him. Was he intent on breaking his neck?

He came to a halt, his gaze intent on Jan herself, walked more slowly, and as he passed her, he seemed to study her intently. Not with the full, insolent, appreciative Roman stare, but certainly more boldly than an Englishman of his type would have scrutinised a stranger.

I sympathise, chum, Jan thought. Dear heaven, I know how you felt. A figure in the distance, the leap of the heart, the hurrying forward with delight. And then the let-down. I was the wrong one, wasn't I? We may not speak each other's language, but love speaks for itself. Being alone isn't fun.

6

In a moment she heard someone running up the Steps and was unable to resist looking back to see if it was the stranger. But it was only a boy, one of those tiresome, irresistibly beautiful Roman urchins, black-haired, with the looks of a Michelangelo and the whining voice of a beggar. She turned away.

Next moment she felt a crippling blow on her elbow. Her arm, momentarily paralysed, dropped; her hand opened. As she staggered to keep her balance, her handbag fell to the ground. The twelve-year-old, he couldn't have been more, swooped and snatched his prize and almost without pause, continued his race up the steps.

Jan called after him, tried to follow. But the sickening pain of her elbow made her weak and dizzy. She sank down and buried her face in her hands. *I'll be all right in a minute*, she thought. *All right in—*

Through a haze, she saw a pair of elegantly-shod feet beside her. Looking up, she saw the man who had gazed at her so inquisitively only a minute or two before. He bent and offered her a hand, addressing her in Italian.

' *Inglesa*,' she told him. ' I don't understand you.' The little Italian she knew was adequate for travelling, but how was she going to explain the awfulness of what had happened to anybody here?

' In that case,' he said, sitting beside her on the Steps, ' we can speak English. I saw what that little brute did. It's an old trick, but they'll go on doing it as long as women insist on carrying a handbag over the arm. It's your own fault. You should be more careful, in a big city.'

She blinked up at him. She felt dangerously near tears, but that wretch had taken even her handkerchief. ' You're blaming *me*?'

' Certainly I am. You dangle those bits of nonsense at the end of two fingers, leading youngsters into

7

temptation. Does the arm feel better now?'

'Thank you.' She had recovered her dignity and was beginning to feel angry. His calm disapproval was adding insult to injury. 'The numbness is wearing off, but the pain is the least of it. I don't know what—' in spite of herself she could not stop the quiver in her voice. 'I don't know what I'm going to do.'

'Did you lose much?'

'Everything.' The enormity of her loss was growing in her mind, now she could think more clearly. 'All my money. Travellers' cheques, return travel tickets, passport—the lot.'

'You were carrying all that about? Here? How can anyone be such a fool? Why didn't you deposit your valuables with the hotel and just carry around what you need from day to day?'

'Why indeed?' she said bitterly. 'My misfortune seems to be annoying you. If you'd have the goodness to direct me to the police station I'll report my loss. Then I suppose I'll have to find the British Consul or someone. At the moment I'm not thinking clearly, but I'll manage by myself, thank you. It was kind of you to speak to me, if only to lecture me on my stupidity.'

'I'll take you to the police. It won't do any good, but you may as well go through the correct procedure.'

'You mean—I'll never get it back?'

'Of course not. Were you naïve enough to think you might? Your bank will replace the travellers' cheques eventually, and the British Consul will do something about your passport and travel documents. It will take a few days, naturally. Come,' he stood up and offered her a hand. 'Since we are going the same way, you may as well ride in my car.' Her hesitation made him smile. 'You are learning discretion, *signorina*? Now you are afraid to trust me? All right. We will leave the car parked, and walk to the *carabinieri*. You'll need an interpreter there; and

8

remember, I am a witness, too.'

She stood up, shook her skirt straight. 'I didn't mean to be rude. Surely your lecture to young women on their own in a foreign city includes the bit about not accepting lifts from strange men?'

'It does.' His voice went icy cold, his gaze flickered over her as if she were something to be swept out of his way. 'If you can think of any way you can manage without me, *signorina*, I shall be delighted to leave you to take it.'

If only there were! But he was so annoyingly right. She needed him, both as witness and interpreter. 'I'm afraid I can't,' she was forced to admit. 'But surely I'm being a nuisance? You were going somewhere in a hurry, when you passed me on your way down.'

'It can wait,' he said carelessly. 'Let us be on our way.'

They used his car after all—a low, long white sports model which he launched into the roaring Roman traffic like an arrow from a bow.

'I'm not surprised your countrymen do so well in international motor-racing,' she ventured. 'You must train them on the streets of Rome. I—*oh*!'

Smiling, he had raced two other cars to get through the narrowing gap between two buses, and won. 'We believe in keeping our traffic moving, *signorina*. The faster the better. We have not the temperament for the slow-stop-slow of your London streets.'

Patiently, he explained her case to the police. They took notes, shrugged, consulted colleagues, talked.

'I can't understand a word,' she confessed to her companion. 'We've been half an hour already. Has anything happened yet?'

'Not a thing. And it won't. They are swamped, poor devils. Our summer tourists are like shoals of silly sardines to our youngsters. Rich pickings from

9

the careless. We couldn't recruit enough
ever to keep track of the handbags and poc
stolen.'

'*Signore*, will you do me one more kindn
two. Stop telling me how silly I am, becau
know. And lend me a handkerchief. I th i
ing to cry.'

He produced a snowy handkerchief of
'No gentleman lends a handkerchief
signorina. I give you mine. Fortunately
been opened.'

She thanked him, having the tact not t
the gift, shook out its cool white folds,
little, which relieved her tenseness. After t
better able to cope, both with the police a
escort.

'And now,' he announced as they left
'you need the British Consul. And, I thin

It took time. A delightful Englishman
and biscuits, talked about his mother in
and sent her away reassured. Fortunate
had been paid in advance for the full tw
all her documents could be replaced with
Her immediate need was for pocket mon
make-up and comb. Lunches and bus
have to be sacrificed until her travellers'
through.

He was waiting, her admonitory
opened the door of his car for her. 'Get
thing all right now?'

'More or less. Except I'm stuck, for a
things come through. But I'll manage fir
You didn't wait for me, did you? I've
ages.'

He was silent a moment. 'We didn't i
selves. My name is Marco Cellini. I liv
an island in the Bay of Naples with my m

10

elderly and sometimes a little confused—and my sister. It seemed to me that unless you have friends here—and as you did not speak of any I assume you have none—your holiday has been spoilt.'

'I wouldn't say that. My confidence is shaken, and for the next few days things will be a bit tricky, but spoilt—oh no.'

'You will find it is so,' he went on as if she had not spoken. 'So I have had an idea. For the next week or two, I need someone to give an eye to my mother occasionally. If you could do that, I would be most happy to offer you the rest of your holiday at my villa. We have our own pool, a boat, an interesting little town, very old. It need not cost you a single lira. What do you say?'

The offer tempted her. He was right, the magic had gone out of Rome. She had almost, without noticing it, grown tired of the incessant noise, the death-dealing traffic, the sleaziness of the city. She had already visited the Vatican and the historic places of antiquity. The thought of a quiet island, a cool pool, a white boat on blue water, was almost beyond refusal.

'Signor Cellini, you have been extraordinarily kind to a stranger today, and to offer me hospitality has added to it. But as you lectured me on prudence, perhaps you'll forgive me if I say it is almost *too* much. We know nothing of each other. Would you think me rude if I told you I would prefer to stay in my hotel? Everything is paid there, except lunches, until the end of my holiday. I really shall be all right there, and I promise you I will take better care of myself and my money in future.'

He nodded. 'I understand. I was prepared to pay you a salary, *signorina*—'

'Janice Lynton. I'm a student nurse in my final year. I live at the Nurses' Hostel.'

He nodded, as if filing the information for future

reference. 'No sweetheart?'

'At the moment, no. I have had boy-friends and I hope to have lots more. But right now, I'm fancy free.' Free? Would she ever be free of Michael and her memories? 'But,' she added swiftly, 'don't think I'm alone in the world. I have heaps of friends.'

'A girl like you would have many friends. Your being a nurse makes me all the more eager to have you. Only till the official end of your holiday. My sister is —away at the moment, so my mother is lonely. She is a little lost in her mind, you see. It is hard to get her to understand why Bianca does not come when she calls.'

'You tempt me, but—'

He produced his card. 'Go back to your nice Englishman and check on my credentials. Please. He will tell you whether I am to be trusted.'

She made a sudden decision. 'No, I'll come, *signore*. I trust you. And I don't want to be paid, thank you. But first I must collect my luggage from the hotel, and leave a forwarding address.'

'Of course.'

The white car leapt into the traffic.

For the second time today, Jan thought as she packed swiftly, I've been a fool. What if the whole thing was a put-up job, urchin and all, to lure me to his island? Why didn't I call his bluff at the Consulate, and go back to check?

There was still the telephone.

'But certainly,' said the friendly Englishman who had given her tea and Marie biscuits. 'Signor Cellini is known to us. He is a wealthy businessman, with interests in Britain. If he has offered you hospitality at his home, with his mother, by all means accept. I'll call you there, when the money and your passport come through. Then if you're not happy, you'll have the wherewithal to back out. All right?'

'Fine.' She replaced the receiver happily. Now for the island, the blue Bay of Naples, the dream villa with the swimming-pool. Was there a catch in it somewhere? The mother might be a great deal pottier than he'd suggested. How much was 'a little lost in her mind'? Well, so be it. She was a nurse, wasn't she? One old lady wouldn't be impossible.

The traffic of Naples was even worse than Rome. Every man drove with his elbow hard down on the horn. The noise was unimaginable, trapped in the narrower streets. It was not until they sank into the luxurious seats of the white hydrofoil which was to take them to Ischia that she felt able to catch her breath.

It was a glorious day, bright and hot. The sea shimmered like blue silk. The hydrofoil skimmed over the water like a bird.

'Another time,' he told her, 'we can take the ferry. You would prefer, perhaps, to be out on a deck?'

'I would. Though this is comfortable, like a sea-borne aeroplane. I wish one could see more of the view. Is that Vesuvius? Can one get to the top?'

He seemed amused. 'Would you want to?'

'But naturally. This is your home, but to me it's all new. Is it possible to visit Pompeii from your island?'

He said rather stiffly, 'If you wish to visit the excavations, I shall take you myself.'

'Oh, please don't put yourself to all that trouble. I'm reasonably capable, although you don't think it. I can potter around happily by myself.'

'I shall escort you,' he said again, as if she had not spoken. It was an order, not an invitation.

They were silent for a while. Then he pointed. 'Capri. See, that blue smudge in the distance? I shall take you there. We can use our own boat.'

'Thank you,' she said mildly. If he wanted to spend his time ferrying her around, why should she object? It was his choice, not hers.

The busy little harbour of Ischia delighted Jan. The hydrofoil was met by a host of mini-taxis and tiny canopied carriages drawn by horses wearing broad white bows of ribbon, scarlet ear-hoods with little bells; some sported a tall white plume on their heads. A row of waterside restaurants reminded her she had not eaten since a scant Continental breakfast soon after half-past seven. Marco Cellini must have noticed her wistful glance.

'You are hungry? Yes, I am sure you are. Wait till I've spoken to my boatman, and we will choose a restaurant. I know the very place.'

The Cellini launch, white with blue trim, was, in fact, moored close to the restaurant he selected. As he pointed it out, his boatman leapt ashore and padded through the crowd on bare brown feet to meet them. His white teeth gleamed in a tan-gold face; his eyes were blue as the Bay. Jan guessed his age at twenty. Wherever did they go, these splendid creatures? All the men she'd seen were coarse-featured, gross of body. Except, of course, her host.

Glancing up at him quickly, she saw him shake his head at the boy, in an emphatic negative. The two spoke in rapid Italian, using their hands in delicate gestures. Then the boy trotted off towards the hydrofoil to collect Jan's cases.

Marco took a table under a red and white awning, out of the sun.

'What would you like to eat, *signorina*?'

'Couldn't you say Jan? I'd feel more at home, please.'

'Very well. You will call me Marco when we are alone, and *signore* before the staff. My mother you will address as *signora*. She may call you anything she

14

fancies; you mustn't mind. I am often my father, my sister, or even myself as a little boy. You understand?' He smiled, begging her sympathy.

'I understand. One gets used to it. Does she repeat herself?'

He sighed, rolled his eyes heavenwards. 'Endlessly.'

'They can't help it, poor darlings. But *signore*—I mean Marco—surely your mother must be young to suffer from this kind of deterioration? You are a young man yourself.'

'It began when my father was drowned. She saw it happen. After that, she lost touch with this world, but never with him. I believe she is happier so. He is always in the next room, or the garden, or the swimming pool. He is more real than we are.'

'She must have loved him very much. What a tragic loss for her.'

'They were completely wrapped up in each other. I hope some day to find a love like that for myself, but I sometimes fear it happens only once in a hundred years.'

'I hope you may be fortunate, Marco. And that you may keep your love longer than she did.'

'Thank you.' He scanned the long menu. 'You will start with asparagus, then grilled chicken with cherries. To follow, an ice. Pistachio?'

She chuckled. 'I may choose my own ice?'

The well-marked eyebrows rose. 'But of course. I asked what you'd like.'

'Correction—you told me. And you were right.'

'I always am,' he informed her coolly.

Over the meal, Marco was a charming companion. It seemed as if he had shed a burden, to become the man he really was. He talked enthusiastically about the island, the village, the harbour, as if he owned the whole place.

'I do, almost,' he admitted when she told him so.

'Apart from the few luxury hotels. When my parents came, there was so little, the people were so poor. We encouraged them to plant luxury crops for the growing tourist trade, installed modern processing methods. Our family brought prosperity of a sort, but now the younger ones want more. They cast envious eyes on Capri and Sorrento.' He made a quick gesture of distaste. 'They can't see those places have lost their identity, their old traditional way of life. People become lazy and greedy when they live by exploiting others.'

'Perhaps the traditional way wasn't a comfortable way, for those who had to live it. Picturesque poverty is great if you're a painter or a photographer. Not if you're enduring it.'

He grimaced. 'A reformer, eh? I must be careful or we'll have tourist markets all over Barini, and an American bar installed in the Villa Tramonti.'

Jan nodded towards the boatboy. 'He's twentieth-century, anyway.'

The boy was stretched flat on his back on the white deck, a transistor set an inch from his ear. Even from the restaurant, they could hear the strains of pop music.

'Dino's father and grandfather were shepherds, leading their flocks. They played pipes made by their own hands. The ancient Romans would have recognised them. Would even our own grandparents recognise Dino?'

'You're a traditionalist, Marco,' she teased. She felt happy and at ease after the unhappy events of the morning, able to laugh with this man who seemed so much more friendly—much younger too—than he had been in Rome.

It seemed her laughter did not please him. He withdrew into his shell. It was as if a cloud had passed across the sun. 'You mean I'm old-fashioned,' he said

16

brusquely. 'I admit it. I admire the old values and virtues, and see no reason why we should throw them overboard just because a few trendy people say so. Honour and decent ways of living have seen mankind through many centuries, and will again. Truth is not changed by calling it old-fashioned.'

She looked down into the enormous green ice-cream the pretty waitress now placed before her. 'You are right, of course, about honour and truth. But surely some things change for the better? People having more to eat, less poverty and better homes. Less work, even. Backbreaking slavery doesn't necessarily make a man good, does it? And aren't we more honest about things now, talk about them more openly?'

'You mean if we call immorality by its proper name we are free to practise it? If we chat happily about dishonesty there's no harm in being dishonest?'

'I didn't mean that, and you know it,' she snapped.

'Then what did you mean?' he pressed her.

He was her host and she did not wish to air views which might spoil the pleasant atmosphere. 'Let's not argue on such a lovely day. I daresay I seem foolish and inexperienced to a man of the world like yourself. You probably disapprove of me in all respects.'

'I probably do,' he said gravely. 'First I disapprove of a young unmarried girl careering round the world alone. One of those famous friends of yours could have accompanied you, surely?'

'I didn't plan to come alone,' she said quickly. 'We'd meant it to be so different.' She had not meant to say as much, and firmly closed her lips on any more disclosures. If Marco disapproved of her travelling alone, still more would he disapprove of the Jan-and-Michael idea. 'And secondly, you are going to tell me, you disapprove of my accepting your invitation?'

'I do.'

Goaded beyond her patience, she tossed her head

proudly. 'I don't find that at all amusing, *signore*. This expedition need go no farther. If you will tell your man to take my cases back to the ferryboat, I will return at once.'

'To Naples? And from Naples to Rome?' There was a ripple of amusement in his tone. 'And where do you propose to find the fares?'

'Since I came at your invitation, to care for your mother, you will pay them. Your old-fashioned ideas of courtesy and fair dealing will compel you to do so, and I shall accept your offer as recompense for my wasted time.'

'Stabbed to the heart!' He placed his hand over his heart as he spoke. 'And with my own weapon. Come, I apologise. You are a nurse and I am sure you came to help my mother, and not for any charms of mine. Am I forgiven for a joke in poor taste?'

She was certain it had not been intended as a joke, but he had offered peace. 'Of course. We belong to different nations, with different attitudes to life, so let us be tolerant of each other.'

'Agreed. Now Dino seems to be ready, so if you have finished that enormous ice-cream, let us be on our way.'

The motor-launch, the *Drusus*, cleaved a white track through the deep blue water. Jan had always loved boats, and was in her element, with the breeze on her face. Now, as Marco Cellini concentrated on handling the fine little craft, she was able to watch him without being noticed. She had found him arrogant, charming, sharp-tongued, kind. A strange mixture. Which was the real man? The face she now studied was a strong one, the fine skin deeply tanned, the chin square, the cheekbones high. She looked with special interest at the mouth, for it is the mouth which betrays the man. Generously wide, yet now the lips were compressed; whether with concentration on his task, or with other thoughts which might, perhaps, have also caused the two sharp frown-lines between the well-marked black eyebrows, she could not tell.

Not, she decided, a happy face. A young one, yet one accustomed to heavy responsibility. A wealthy businessman, her English friend had said on the telephone. So it might be the cares of wealth or international business which weighed on him now.

After twenty minutes, Dino touched her arm, smiled and pointed.

' Barini, *signorina*.'

Marco glanced over his shoulder. ' Little more than a lump of volcanic rock, but men have made a home of sorts on it for a few thousand years. The harbour is round the other side.'

The side they approached was steep, rising straight out of the sea without a beach or rocks at the base. Jan craned her neck to the summit of the crag, where a thin layer of soil and green growth clung precariously. All the way down, it was possible to see the rock formations, the slits and cracks, the caves eaten by the everlasting sea. Once or twice, Dino pointed to where lava must once have flowed, molten rock like treacle and now set hard as granite.

Jan shuddered. A cruel home, but well defended. Not only a home for shepherds, she guessed, but a lair of pirates well placed for a foray.

Round on the other side there was a different story. This was the fair face of Barini, with gardens running down the cliffs, and beaches lipped by shallow emerald waters. The tiny harbour built of dressed stone, the tiny lighthouse, were toylike. A man and some boys sat fishing on the end of the pier, but leapt to their feet shouting and waving as the launch came in silently. Dino waved back.

' Wave to them, Jan,' Marco barked. He was intent on bringing his boat to its mooring, but he had given an order. Obediently, she waved. After all, he was master of this craft and entitled to bark orders.

The approach to the villa was up a narrow road which ascended in breathtaking hairpin bends to the highest point of the island. They used a beach-buggy, painted lemon-yellow and having a pink candy-striped awning. The unlikely little vehicle packed a lot of power, and Marco's muscular brown hands twisted it this way and that, as deftly as he had handled the boat. And at last, under a white archway, they came to the garden of the Villa Tramonti.

'Home,' said Marco, smiling at her.

She smiled in return. 'It's always nice to come home?'

To her dismay, the innocent question wiped the smile from his face. For a brief moment, unutterable sadness looked out of those searching eyes, and touched the strong mouth. Then he brought the smile back and spoke.

'Of course. Don't you find it so?' But the voice was the voice of a stranger once more.

To enter the house, one passed along an arched white corridor; one side was open to the sea, each opening framed with flowers. Geraniums scarlet and pink; cascades of purple bougainvillaeas, and, to Jan's delight, a riot of colourful homely sweet williams. At the end of the arcade, framed by the brilliance of the distant sea, there was a bronze statue of a seated boy over a little fountain which sparkled as it rose and fell into a marble basin encircled by alabaster doves.

The door was black and heavily carved, set in a white arch within an arch of gold mosaic. A huge white bowl of pink geraniums was set on either side.

'But it is quite, quite beautiful, Marco.'

'Thank you. My father created it, out of an old tumbledown house he bought for the sake of the site. He and my mother made it a life's work.'

He led her through a cool dark entrance hall, through glass doors into what seemed to be the main room of the villa. It was large and cool, built after the ancient Roman fashion round an open courtyard with a circular pool and another fountain. Banks of lilies grew round the pool, filling the air with their fragrance.

The floor was white marble, in which were reflected six pendant crystal chandeliers, and the comfortable-looking chairs and sofas, all upholstered in pale blue. Round the white walls, Jan observed six tall black marble plinths, each supporting a fine marble bust. It surprised her that a room so pure in line, so simple —almost austere—could at the same time look so supremely luxurious.

She had fallen on her feet. To spend the rest of her holiday in this glorious place was something of which she had not dreamed. She now saw the Rome hotel for what it was—fair enough, for those who wanted a holiday without breaking the bank, and didn't mind roughing it a bit. But noisy, over-full, gone down in the world since the palmy days of the Edwardian travelling English.

'Do you like it?' Marco asked, with a rather touching pride.

'Very much.' She looked around curiously. 'But why don't you have a view? I'd want huge windows looking over the sea.'

'And you'd find out your mistake. With you, the sun is a rare friend. Here he can be an enemy. The sea is all around us, and we spend much of our time outside, where we get all the light and warmth we can take. Then we have a retreat into shade and coolness.'

'Yes, I see. Another difference in outlook.'

A tall slim lady came towards them, drifting over the white floor like a ghost. She was dressed entirely in black, her skirt touching the floor and a black lace mantilla on her white hair. A peasant dress, made by a master hand in superb material, Jan guessed.

'Marco! Oh, my dear boy, how lovely to see you. Your father will be delighted. He was saying only this morning how long you'd been away. Is this your dear wife? Bless you, dear. My daughter will be pleased to have a sister.'

'This is Jan Lynton, Mother. She is English. You must speak English to her, dear.'

'That's charming. I never thought you'd marry an English girl, my son.'

The Signora's Italian was so pure, her speech so clear and correct, that Jan had been able to follow the conversation fairly well. It did not embarrass her in the least to be thought Marco's wife. Hospital life quickly cured one of any nonsense like that. But she thought it had embarrassed the man.

She whispered quickly, 'It's all right, I understand. Please don't mind on my account.'

He flashed her a grateful look. 'But we must make her understand.' He turned to his mother again. 'Jan is a guest, Mother. Not my wife.'

'Of course not. I know very well you're not married. She has come to visit Bianca.' Then she said to Jan in perfect English, 'You are most welcome, child. My daughter gets lonely, up on this great rock. Run along and talk to her. You'll find her in the swimming pool.'

Marco tensed. 'Mother, think. *Is Bianca here?*'

'Where else? This is her home.'

'Excuse me, Jan.' He raced across the room and out through a porticoed door at the end. In a moment he was back. Catching Jan's eye, he spread his expressive hands and shrugged, mouthing *Not there*.

'Bianca is on holiday, Mother,' he explained carefully. 'You remember, she has gone to visit Aunt Giulia-Maria in Florence. Jan is to use her rooms, and she's very tired after her journey. Will you show her where to go?'

Signora Cellini gave Jan a serene smile and led the way.

'I'll come too,' Marco murmured, ' or who knows where you may be led? You see what I mean? She's safe and happy here, and needs no nursing or anything like that. It is companionship she lacks, and normally Bianca is with her.'

'Signor Marco, I'll be truly happy to be with her. I see my Italian will improve, listening to her. This is a perfectly heavenly place and I think I am lucky to be here. Thank you for such a kind thought. Few people would have had the imagination to realise that that sordid little incident would spoil the taste of the rest of my holiday. I'm afraid I haven't thanked you properly for your thoughtfulness.'

'If you do so, you'll embarrass me. I was at my wits' end to know where I should find exactly the right person. When I first set eyes on you, it was like a miracle.'

She frowned, remembering. 'But that was before my purse was stolen. You ran towards me as if you knew me, then suddenly checked yourself. As a matter of fact, I thought you'd taken me for—for a friend.'

He did not answer for a moment. The route lay across the garden, skirting an oblong swimming pool lined with blue tiles and edged with marble.

'I'm sorry about that,' he said at last. 'You would think me rude. The fact is, I was worrying away to myself and then suddenly I thought I saw Bianca herself walking towards me. You're the same height and —er—shape. Your colouring, too. Now I see you more closely, the resemblance is only slight, but at a distance it was remarkable. So naturally I hurried to meet my sister—till I was near enough to see I'd been mistaken.'

So that was it. And I had thought, from the blazing joy on his face, that he'd been running to meet a girl he loved.

'I see. I thought perhaps you'd taken me for your girl-friend. You must be awfully fond of Bianca.'

'We all are,' he said gravely.

'These are Bianca's rooms.' Her hostess turned to Jan, and had not forgotten to speak in English. 'Please feel at home here. She'll be back in a minute. Do you play the guitar?'

Jan smiled. 'Who doesn't? I'm not particularly good, but I keep practising.'

'Bianca isn't very good either. You must practise together. I'll go and tell my husband you are here.'

Marco led her farther inside. 'This is her sitting-room. Please feel free to use anything you find here. I'd be delighted if you'd continue your guitar practice. We're all so used to it now, the Villa wouldn't be the same without it. Her bedroom is through there, bathroom and all you'll need.'

'Thank you. I hope she won't mind my using all her things. Some girls wouldn't like to have a stranger doing that.'

'Bianca is the soul of hospitality, I assure you. Now I want you to behave exactly as if this were your home. Ring for a servant if you want anything—anything at all. Perhaps you'd like a *spremuta* now?'

'What's that?'

'Oranges freshly squeezed into a tall glass, and topped up with ice.'

'I'd adore one.'

'Ring the bell and order. And Jan—there's one special thing I would like you to do while you are our guest. It's very simple.'

'Then of course I'll do it.'

'Wear Bianca's clothes. Everything is Italian or

24

French and is sure to fit you. She has a hoard of swim suits too.'

She stared in astonishment. 'Oh no! I couldn't do that!'

'You promised. And why not? Don't pretty girls like dressing up? And you are a remarkably pretty girl, Jan. You'd look marvellous in the sort of things Bianca wears.'

'She may be the soul of hospitality, but you're a man. You must be crazy to think her sense of hospitality would extend to having me rummage in her wardrobe and dress in her clothes.'

The cold voice spoke. The must-be-obeyed voice of the master of this house. 'I know my sister, *signorina*. Please do as I say.' He turned and strode away across the garden without another word.

A young maid arrived, and at the second try Jan made her understand what she wanted. Like her mistress, the girl wore an ankle-length black skirt, made youthful and pretty by the addition of a white lace-edged apron, a full-sleeved white blouse with a narrow black velvet ribbon bow. On her smooth black hair she had a white lace headdress with red ribbons down to her shoulders.

The girl smiled, nodded, and ran off. Jan continued her thoughtful tour of Bianca's apartments. What sort of girl was it, who didn't mind a stranger wearing her clothes?

A shiver ran down Jan's spine. Did Bianca really exist? Or was she a figment of the Signora's imagination—a sort of ghost?

A very modern ghost, then. Bianca kept herself up to date. The inevitable pile of pop records. Hi-fi equipment—very, *very* lush. A pile of subtly coloured sandals, tumbled as if the owner were in the habit of rummaging through for what she fancied; those were this year's style or well ahead of it. Fine Italian work.

On a marble table, carelessly put down, wing-sided sunglasses.

In the bedroom, it was the same. Jan opened a long row of fitted wardrobes and handled the exquisite garments hung there. Your brother is both rich and generous, Bianca, she thought. I'd love to see myself in some of these creations, and if you really mind about it, have your quarrel with him, not me. He made me promise.

Here, there really was a sea-view. Long windows opened on to a balcony with a sheer drop below. Leaning over made Jan clutch the rail and close her eyes. So far down there, so emerald the water!

Between the two tall windows, there stood a gilt table topped with glass. On the table, a small, exquisite white kid beauty box, fully fitted. After her own loss of the morning, not yet replaced, Jan was truly tempted. Everything was here. Powders, lipsticks in a dozen colours, eye-liners and shadows, mascara. Thoughtfully, her gaze still on the lavish array, Jan reached for the tiny perfume bottle and sniffed. Um, lovely! A famous name adorned the jewel-like bottle.

Something wrong here. What was it?

Remembering how bereft she'd felt earlier in the day, when all her make-up, modest as it was, disappeared with her money, Jan knew—and shivered.

What sort of girl goes on a long visit and leaves her beauty box at home?

CHAPTER II

Jan sank down on to a low white leather stool, her eyes fixed on the beauty box. It was possible that Bianca had a smaller version she used for travelling and had taken a few of her favourite cosmetics with her. Yet these had such an air of being used and loved. Only a girl could know how another girl would sit over such a well-filled box, choosing among her treasures as lovingly as if they had been diamonds, rubies, emeralds.

If Bianca had been feminine enough to spend time and money choosing such a collection, she was feminine enough to want it with her.

A cold shiver touched Jan's spine. Had Marco Cellini's young sister died recently and suddenly? Did she now inhabit that dream world of her mother's? It was not possible to forget that casual *You'll find her in the swimming pool*—nor Marco's strange amazement. Yet he had hurried to see if she really was in the pool. He wouldn't have done so, if he'd known her to be dead.

I'm making mountains out of molehills, she decided at last. How do I know how the very rich live, or how they regard their possessions? This Bianca may have a dozen beauty cases, a hundred lipsticks, for all I know. And why should she care who wears her clothes? I'll bet she has more new dresses in a month than any of us in the Nurses' Hostel gets in five years. What I need is a shower, a cloud of that heavenly scented talc, and something new to wear.

The bathroom was floored in black marble. Jan threw off her clothes and ran across it, seeing the dim shape of her body deeply reflected. A warm shower rinsed away the stress and heat of her day; then, as she cautiously turned it to cold, the water came through more strongly, stinging like needles till she tingled with energy.

Then there was the delightful business of choosing a new dress. Or, she thought, riffling through the vast wardrobe, trouser suit; for Bianca had an elegant line in those.

Finally she chose a cornflower blue fitted cotton blouse with deeply cuffed sleeves, and wide flaring trousers to match. From a drawerful of carelessly tangled costume jewellery she took a pale blue beaded choker, and three broad white bangles.

The result pleased her, as she peacocked before the long mirrors. Say what you like, she grimaced at her own image, expensive clothes do something for a girl. Her feet were bare, but a pair of sugar-pink and white high-heeled sandals took care of that. After some experimentation with Bianca's make-up, she produced the gentle, translucent effect she had admired in others but so far rarely managed to produce for herself. A delicate shading of eye-shadow completed the picture.

H'm, dreamy, Jan thought, scrutinizing her face critically in a hand-mirror. No wonder she uses that most; it must be just her colour, as it is mine.

Now she was ready to face the Villa Tramonti and whatever it might contain. She hesitated only a second or two, with the jewelled perfume flask in her hand, then put it down. Not that. I may drift around here looking like Bianca Cellini, but I'm dashed if I'm going to *smell* like her. The cold shiver touched her spine again.

The maid returned, with the orange drink on a tiny silver tray. When she saw Jan she uttered an exclamation of pleasure. Then, recognising the visitor wearing her mistress's clothes, the girl's face darkened with anger. Her eyes darted from the wardrobe to Jan, and back to the wardrobe. If she had not been so well trained, Jan knew, she would have protested strongly. As it was, she tossed her head and marched out of the room, expressing in every line of her plump little body the indignation she so clearly felt.

She'll tell the others and they'll hate me. Cool glass in hand, Jan wandered through to the sitting-room. Did an invitation to play the guitar extend to an invitation to use the record player? Hesitation disappeared when the sulky, handsome face of her favourite singer glowered at her from the sleeve at the top of the pile. She put the record on, lowered the volume discreetly, stretched herself upon an elegant chaise-longue and crossed her ankles.

This was the life! And all for free.

The warm sensuous throbbing of a familiar male voice, the cool comfortable room, the sense of complete detachment from the real world outside, made Jan realise how deeply tired she was. Since setting out for Rome she had walked every day quite as far as she ever walked in the wards, and mostly over cobbled roads. The heat and incessant noise outside, the dark museums and churches packed with so many treasures that the mind reeled—it had all drained her energy. Providence, no less, had made that impudent urchin snatch her bag. Ten days of this, and she'd go back to the hospital full of vitality and rarin' to go.

She fell asleep, and woke to find the Signora Cellini looking down at her.

'Sleeping, my love? How lovely you looked—like a child. It's almost time for dinner.'

Jan scrambled up. 'Thank you, *signora*. I've had a difficult day, one way and another, so I just dropped off. Were you needing me?'

The delicate hand cupped her chin for a moment. 'Bianca dear, I always need you.'

Firmly, Jan said, 'I am not your daughter, *signora*. I'm Jan—a visitor.'

Troubled, Bianca's mother said uncertainly, 'Oh, I

thought—aren't you Bianca?'

'You know I'm not. You're talking English. You don't speak to your daughter in English, do you?'

'I'm sorry, I made a mistake. Yes, yes, I see now you are someone else. Jan?'

'Jan Lynton. Bianca is visiting her Aunt Giulia-Maria.'

'So she is,' discovered Signora Cellini. 'Never mind. You and I will enjoy ourselves. You shall improve my English and I will improve your Italian. Now come, let us eat. Do you know my son is home? He brought his wife. He lives in Rome nowadays, but today he is home. Take my hand.'

They found Marco in a small dining-room whose floor was tiled with yellow and white tiles. Here tall windows opened on to a terrace facing the sea, and long white filmy curtains moved in the almost imperceptible current of air, creating an atmosphere of fresh coolness.

He bowed over her hand, touched it with his lips. 'Ah—a young goddess! May I congratulate you, *signorina*. You look perfect, dressed as you are, a hundred times more like Bianca. That is very delightful.'

'In her clothes, I should look like her. They fit perfectly, so you were right about size. One thing I must ask you, *signore*—' she glanced at his mother and dropped her voice. 'Please tell the servants you invited me to wear your sister's clothes. That little maid—'

'Francesca?'

'She was furious. Not that she said anything, but her face spoke volumes. She'll tell the others I've been helping myself, and they will hate me for it.'

'I'm sorry. Trust me, I'll explain. I shall say you were the victim of a thief.'

'You don't have to do this for me, you know. I have

clothes of my own.'

He said gravely, ' But you have to do it for me. You promised.'

After dinner they sat on the terrace, a family three-some, relaxed, not talking much. But when the tele-phone rang, Marco jumped as if he had been tensed and waiting. He came back like a man who has had ill news.

' Who was it, my son? Was it Bianca? She's on holiday just now, in Florence.'

You remember better than you pretend, Jan thought. How much is genuine, how much an act for Marco's benefit? Perhaps even for your own.

' Just a business call, Mother. Jan, how would you like to play to us?'

She shrugged. ' I'm not good enough for a public performance.'

' We're not critics. Shall I fetch the guitar?'

Bianca's was a beautiful instrument. Jan enjoyed using it, and soon forgot her self-consciousness, even sang a little, under her breath, till memories of Michael got between her and the music and choked her into silence.

' Thank you,' said the Signora, rising. ' I shall go to bed now. My husband likes to retire early these days. He's not well, not really well. Goodnight, my son. Goodnight, Jan.'

Marco escorted his mother to her room. When he returned, he asked what Jan thought of her.

' She's lovely—a great lady of the old time. I've never met one before, and I'm impressed. But, Marco, you really ought to try to do something about her memory. She's not so confused as she makes out. When she was pretending I was Bianca, she was speak-ing all the time in English. She knew who I was, you see.'

' Are you criticising my mother? Saying she tells

lies?'

'Goodness, no, nothing like that.'

'It sounded like that.'

'All I'm saying is, she's in trouble and she could be cured. Well, improved anyway. I don't think you do her a kindness, letting her indulge in this play-acting. Why don't you tell her your father is dead?'

'Why awaken her to a cruel world and a bitter grief?'

'Because this is the real world, and she's living in it. You're treating her as if she were a ghost.'

'So now I am coming under your hammer? You are no more than a student nurse, you told me? Are you setting yourself up against the opinions of the greatest doctors in Europe?'

Jan crimsoned. 'I'm sorry if I seemed cheeky. Did you have a woman doctor?'

'No. Why?'

She shrugged. 'A truly beautiful, feminine woman can always fool a man, rarely a woman. I think you ought to be sure how much of her mental condition is real, how much is pretence on her part; and how much you yourself are responsible for.'

'I?' His face was dark with anger.

'Yes, you. You keep things from her—like not letting her remember her husband died. Every day you go along with her fantasy, you make it more real for her. But what if you died? Got drowned, as he did? It happens. What would become of her then? You have no right to keep a human being as a sort of Sleeping Beauty.'

'No *right*? I am the master of this household. I have every right. You as my guest have no right—if I may respectfully remind you—to call my treatment of my mother into question.'

'No, I haven't,' she admitted quietly. 'And I apologise. But I may respectfully remind you that you did ask me what I thought. Why ask questions, if you don't want any answers?'

Sky and sea were violet now, after the sunset. He moved abruptly to the edge of the balcony and stared down. Presently he said in a normal voice,

'Come here, Jan.' She went to him. He pointed to a headland far below, a dark diamond shape jutting out into the sea. 'See that light? It's a castle. You'll see it by daylight plainly enough. It has been made habitable, and is occupied by a very old friend of our family. He is Bianca's godfather and fond of her. When he sees her up here, he likes to wave. If he does so, it would be kind of you to wave back.'

'Another fantasy? You want to make him believe I'm Bianca?'

He turned to look at her. When he spoke, there was no rancour in his tone. 'Is that wrong? He is old and lonely. It's a game they play, and if it gives him pleasure, surely you can co-operate.'

'It's a silly game. Suppose Bianca writes to him, sends him a postcard, while she's away?'

'She is not likely to.'

'Why?'

'Because I say so. Don't ask so many questions. If you don't want to make the old man happy for a few moments each day, then don't. Let him feel lonely. He's used to it.'

'I'll do it. If he's so lonely, why not pop down for a chat?'

'It's ten miles by the road, and while I'm at the Villa I need to be near the telephone. I'm expecting an urgent call—business.'

'Goodness! Is that what being a tycoon means? You can't leave the house at all?'

'Not till I've had this call. So you'll wave?'

She relented. Why be critical? These people weren't her family, nor her patients. She had no

33

responsibility for them, beyond the normal courtesies of a guest. Then at least she should accept her position as guest, and fall in with her host's wishes.

' I'll wave. Trust me.'

He touched her elbow lightly. ' Good girl! Thank you. Now I'll follow my mother and retire. I've been missing some sleep lately and it is beginning to tell. I breakfast at seven here on the terrace. Ring when you're ready for yours. Goodnight, English Jan. Have a happy time and feel this is your home.'

For dinner, he had changed into a white suit which, even more than that which he had worn in Rome, showed off his broad shoulders and slim waist. One day soon, she thought, I'll see him in a swim suit and he will look like a Greek god and that golden tan of his will be all-over. He will be perfectly muscled and swim like a fish. If he wasn't so bad-tempered and touchy, he'd be perfect.

The night was too warm, too beautiful to leave. The moon rode high. The scents of the garden were heavier now; lilies, the vanilla scent of broom and the long white bracts of acacia blossom. Jan stretched out on the deep cushions of a long cane chair, and sighed contentedly. The nurses at the hostel would never believe a word of this.

You're making it up, Jan! But go on! What was he like?

Dreamy, she'd tell them. Dark eyes, almost black. Dark hair, a strong face, a voice like dark brown velvet. And charming. He kissed my hand.

Someone would giggle, *I don't believe you!*

True every word. And at night, when it was dark and warm, we'd swim in the pool among the scent of lilies. Jan smiled at her fancy. That wasn't true, but it would be fun to swim in the dark. Why not?

When she came back wearing her own turquoise halter-neck bikini, and trailing a huge pink and orange towel, she heard from somewhere in the house the shrill of a telephone. Marco's business call? Or maybe Bianca calling her family. She froze a moment, but as the ringing stopped and no one seemed to stir from the house, she sat on the marble edge of the pool and slid gently in. The water was warm after the long hot day.

She swam the length of the pool. The disturbed water shone silver. Then she floated, resting on the water and staring at the great star-studded arch of sky. Her hair spread out like a fan.

Someone came running up the garden steps. Hearing the pad of feet, she pulled her own under her and glided to the side of the pool, hoping not to be noticed and keeping her head just below the rim. A terracotta jar of lilies would, she hoped, conceal her completely until the intruder had gone.

Lights were switched on. Marco, again wearing his town suit, hurried out and met the newcomer. It was the boy from the boat, Dino. They talked together in low voices.

'The boat, Dino. Quickly.'

That much Jan understood. And then *Roma*. Was he going to Rome tonight? She knew his car was garaged on the mainland, and he had refuelled before they left it. What had called him back so late? His business call? Was this one of the penalties of being an international tycoon; the price of being wealthy?

The two were talking fast now. She could not understand a word, so was in no danger of eavesdropping. But as Dino turned away, he hesitated and spoke again.

'*E la signorina?*'

He had seen her! Jan gripped the marble edge of the pool, annoyed with herself for skulking under the lilies. How foolish she was going to look!

But Marco said something quickly to the boy, and

ran lightly back into the villa. Jan sighed with relief.

Dino nodded and went away. But as he went, he must have noticed the big towel lying, for he came back, folded it neatly, and carried it away, as if it were all in the day's work to find discarded possessions strewn around the pool.

In the morning Jan chose a sun-suit in a multi-coloured Hawaiian print and scarlet sandals. She breakfasted alone on the terrace. Fresh orange juice, warm rolls with butter and cherry jam, and a great pot of coffee. It was served by Francesca, the plump maid, who smiled and seemed to accept that this guest wore the Signorina Bianca's clothes. Presently Jan heard her talking to a man, and when the pair of them came into the garden she saw it was Dino. So he had brought the boat back? Had Marco come too?

Dino flashed his broad grin. Wearing his usual gear of faded blue jeans and a gold cross on a chain which flashed against his bare brown chest, he bowed as gracefully as a mediaeval page, and handed her a letter with a flourish.

It was from Marco. 'I have been called away on business,' it read. 'I could not wait, as it is urgent. It is not possible to say how long I shall be away, but I hope not too long. Do not let my mother worry, keep her amused if you can. Dino will take you anywhere you want to go, but it would not be wise to wander off on your own. You might get lost, and our cliffs are high and dangerous.'

Not much, but he had remembered her in the haste of his night journey. The disappointment she felt surprised her. In his absence, her visit lacked the spice of excitement—danger, almost—it had had yesterday.

The Signora came out. She was dressed in pink linen, her white hair coiled elegantly on the top of her head. 'Good morning, *signorina*. I hope you slept

36

well?'

'Thank you, madam, I slept wonderfully. It is so quiet here, after a Rome hotel.'

She knows me. No nonsense about Bianca. I'm right, I know I'm right. Half her trouble is because people don't bother to tell her things. And in having nothing to do, no object in life.

'Signor Marco has returned to Rome,' she ventured, wondering what the response would be.

Marco's mother sat down and stared out to sea. 'He comes and goes. He is always busy, that one.' She seemed to take it for granted that Jan was wearing a sun-suit belonging to her daughter. Or did not notice.

'*Signora*, you promised me an Italian lesson. Is it convenient now?'

'Why not? Fetch my embroidery, child, and we can begin.'

Jan had no idea where to find the embroidery, but rang for Francesca and quickly made the girl understand, by gestures, what she required. Marco's mother was a good teacher and seemed to enjoy Jan's company, but after half an hour the girl called a halt. 'You must not tire yourself. What do you do in the mornings, *signora*?'

'Go round the gardens with my husband.'

Jan stood up and took the fine linen embroidery away. 'But since your husband is not here today, will you go round with me?'

'But naturally. You are our guest. Come and see.' Without further comment, her hostess led Jan round the pool and into the garden proper.

The tour took time. There were so many corners, so many plants, and the Signora knew each one and what it needed. Flowers flowed like fountains from the walls, from tall white plant-stands. There were miniature rock gardens, and banks of ferns clustered round tiny fountains. The garden was so much part of the house, and the house part of the garden, that one could not always be sure whether one was indoors or out. Sometimes there was a view of the sea, and sometimes of the mountains. Up flights of steps, down into secret grottoes each with its stone deity and often a stone seat too. The Signora was tireless, drawn on and on by her enthusiasm, her love for every growing thing.

'This is my husband's favourite,' she said so many times, and always with a glowing smile. But never, Jan noticed, did she expect her husband to appear. She was not looking for him. They were together in spirit only. It was the happiest hour of her day, Jan was convinced.

Reluctantly, she found herself agreeing with Marco. It would be cruel to sever this delicate link.

At last they came out on to a terrace, where chairs were set out, and a white wrought-iron table. The terrace overhung the sea on the harbour side of the island and dominated the view with a larger-than-life white statue of some Roman emperor set on the corner. Far below, Jan could see the busy little harbour, the bright coloured fishing boats, the gaily decorated horse-carriages; all looked like toys. Her companion sat down, with a little sigh as if her long walk had exhausted her. She pointed to a silver bell on the table, which Jan rang. Francesca appeared at once, with a tray of cool drinks and some almond cakes. Plainly this was a regular routine and the girl had been waiting for her mistress.

As they rested, Jan asked the Italian for harbour. *Il porto*. She memorized the word carefully. After the siesta, she would ask Dino to take her down there in the beach buggy, to buy postcards and perhaps find a few presents and souvenirs which would be different from the usual tourist trash.

'There's an orange tree!' she exclaimed suddenly. 'With oranges and blossom at the same time. I mean

38

to make a list of all the things you have in this astonishing garden. But right now, I'm going to laze under it.'

The Signora smiled at her guest's enthusiasm. 'We planned the orange trees together, my husband and I. This was a bare rock when we began.'

Jan dragged her chair under the tree and tilted it till she could stare up through the fruit and flowers, and the sun filtered through the leaves.

'Why don't you go on planning?'

'At my age? It's too late. I would never see a new garden flower.'

'For your grandchildren.'

'I have none.'

Jan sat up again. 'That's no way for a gardener to talk. One plants for one's children's children, and you have Signor Marco and the Signorina Bianca. They will marry and they will have children. You could have a fountain with a baby, like the Moses fountain on the Pincine Hill in Rome. It would be the first of your grandchildren, but not the last.'

'A new garden? I wonder where? There is the fern garden, we always meant to make that better. Fountains are difficult, here on the top of the rock. But a statue, that would be easy. I'll speak to my husband about it.'

'Speak to your son.'

The lady looked up sharply, with a strangely cunning smile. She knows, Jan decided suddenly. She's perfectly aware that it's Marco who is the head of the family now.

'I'll think about it. I'd forgotten the ideas we had for the fern garden. Perhaps Marco's wife will help me.'

'I didn't know he was married.' Jan felt a sudden shock of dismay. She had assumed, perhaps rashly, that the talk of Marco's wife yesterday had been of no

39

significance; one of those mistakes confused minds can make. But what if he really did have a wife somewhere?

She lay back and squinted up through the orange leaves. So what? It's of no importance to me. Except, of course, that an unmarried man is always more interesting to a girl than a married one. And he really *is* rather a charmer, in spite of being so touchy.

Could I fall in love with him? He possesses terrific physical attraction, and he would know how to charm a woman if he tried. Instinctively she knew he would be more experienced, more passionate, more demanding than any of the boys she'd known. A woman could be wax in his hands. And if, added to physical passion, there should prove to be that affinity of soul and heart which alone can turn desire into deep and lasting love, he could know the sort of glorious marriage of which he dreamed. A marriage for all eternity, as his father and mother had known. Two dear lovers whom even death could not entirely divide.

I could fall in love with him, she decided, if he wanted me to. He could make any woman love him. But it would be a tragedy if he did not love in return, for having loved Marco Cellini, how could anyone be satisfied with another?

The Signora had dozed lightly, upright in her chair. Softly, Jan got up and prowled round this eyrie so high above the sea. The sheer drop was carefully guarded by elegant white rails, but in the farthest corner she found a gate which opened on to the rock and a narrow staircase leading down.

Interested, she leaned over to see where it led, but it quickly curved away and disappeared. Too dangerous, perhaps? But there was a handrail of sorts, so it must have been used once. Perhaps when Marco was a boy his feet would go flying down here, without any sense of danger? Because, unless it ended in some little ledge, with perhaps an old seat, just another view-point, that path must eventually come down on the shore. There might be a private beach.

Cautiously she pushed the gate. It opened silently on oiled hinges. If she could just peer round the corner—

It was not as difficult as she had feared. The hand-holds had been renewed, and the steps were in good repair. Like everything else she had seen at the Villa Tramonti, this staircase was cared for, even if no one used it now. At the corner she saw its continuation. It did, indeed, go all the way down to a narrow white beach, with the sea over the sand emerald and turquoise, and a tiny thumbnail of white foam on the edge.

It would be easy enough to get down, if one were careful. The return not so easy, being so steep; but possible. Although there were shrubs, and clumps of magenta valerian, the steps were not overgrown. Maybe Bianca used it. Tomorrow, Jan decided, I'll go down and swim in the sea; the real thing, turquoise and emerald and azure.

Lunch was a featherlight pizza, with anchovies and olives. And after lunch the Villa Tramonti retired for the siesta, and Jan began to feel a touch of boredom. All Bianca's books were Italian, and it was too hot to study. Siesta might be a good idea after all.

She woke about four, and went in search of Dino. The boy was gardening, but when Jan said firmly, ' Il porto, per favore,' he grinned cheerfully and trotted off, indicating that he would bring the buggy to the main archway soon. His idea of soon being Italian and not British, Jan was there first. She was wearing her own dress and sunhat, feeling it would not be right to appear amongst the islanders in Bianca's distinctive clothes. She planned to spend a long time wandering round the harbour and small village, and there seemed

41

to be a Byzantine church which might repay exploration. So when Dino at last arrived, she smiled happily and climbed in beside him.

' *Il porto*, Dino?'

' *Si, si, signorina.*'

Certain that the boy understood she wanted the harbour, Jan made no comment when he started away uphill instead of down. No doubt he knew what he was doing. Before long they emerged on to a lonely coastal road, with magnificent views of the headlands and the sea. From the road almost down to the water's edge, cascades of flowering broom fell like rivers of gold.

Dino grinned. *'Bella, bella!'* He waved a hand proudly, as if he had himself laid out the road and the view.

A coastal road would, in time, lead to the harbour, so Jan agreed happily and settled down to enjoy Dino's conducted tour. He stopped at a village and invited her to walk around. The houses, heaped together like a box of spilled bricks, were white or blue, yellow or Pompeiian red, but she was shocked by the dirt and all too obvious poverty. One house was built of ragged lumps of old concrete cemented together crudely. The roof consisted of terracotta drainpipes stacked six deep and covered in cement. There was no proper door and Jan felt pretty sure the floor was trodden earth. Goats and children played around the front of this shack. She shuddered, thinking the only good feature of the village was the fresh sea air and constant sunshine.

Returning to the buggy, she said again firmly that she wished to go to the harbour. He gave his usual happy nod, and set off at a reckless speed over the bumpy road. Half an hour later, after a breathtakingly lovely drive round the coast, he drew up triumphantly and waved a hand towards an ancient castle perched high on a solitary rock. '*Castello!*' Then, turning and pointing to the heights from which they had descended, 'Villa Tramonti.'

This must be, then, the castle visible from the Villa, where Bianca's godfather lived, and from which he waved sometimes to the girl. Shading her eyes, she stared up till she located the roof of the Villa.

Time was getting on, and although she felt sure Dino was doing his best to give her an enjoyable outing, she began to feel irritated by her failure to reach the harbour and the few shops she had seen there. By now they must be a long way from home and there would be little time for the souvenir-hunting.

'Dino,' she said loudly and clearly in English, more than half convinced that he could understand, 'I want to go to the harbour. Boats. Harbour.' Suddenly she remembered the name of Marco's boat. 'The *Drusus*. Take me to the *Drusus*.'

'Ah!' Understanding lit the boy's face. '*Drusus? Si, si, signorina.*'

'If you say *si, si* again and don't take me there, Dino, I will strangle you with my own hands!'

Another five minutes and the buggy jerked to another stop. They were as high above the harbour as ever. Dino leaned over a stone wall, pointing.

'*Drusus, signorina!*'

Jan began to giggle. What an absurd afternoon! She had credited Dino with more understanding than the poor boy possessed, or her Italian was much worse than she had realised. Seeing her laughter, Dino laughed too.

'*Bella?*'

The view certainly was beautiful, even though the harbour was as far out of reach as ever. 'Tomorrow, Dino, we'll try again. Let's go home now. Villa Tramonti.'

He nodded. 'Villa Tramonti.' Then he jabbed a

finger towards the port. ' *Il porto.*'

How could she destroy his pride of achievement? ' Thank you, Dino. *Grazie.*'

In the cool drawing room of the Villa, the mistress of the house was sitting with her embroidery. She looked up, smiled, and calling Jan Bianca, spoke to her in Italian.

Back to Square One!

Early next morning Jan put on one of Bianca's bikinis, and her own trusty shoes. Then, with towel and sandals slung round her neck, she slipped away to find the steps down to that secret beach she coveted. She had a great longing to swim in the sea, and an even greater longing to be alone.

The gate was padlocked.

She felt sick with shock. That padlock definitely wasn't there yesterday.

Yesterday she had walked through the gate and tested the path. Had someone seen her, and decided she was not to go down that way? If the steps were unsafe, surely the Signora could have told her? Who had made the decision—and why that heavy chain?

Dino had frustrated her desire to go down to the harbour yesterday. Was that lack of understanding, in such an apparently sensible and trusted young man? Or had it been done on purpose?

If so, did it tie up with the locking of the gate which effectively prevented her getting down to the beach?

' In other words,' she said aloud, staring back at the silent garden, ' is someone trying to keep me a prisoner here?'

CHAPTER III

Jan sat on the warm stone, the morning sun across her shoulders, and stared into the azure distance, thinking hard. She hugged her knees and sat so still that presently a tiny green lizard flicked out from a crack and sunned itself beside her, the minute throat pulsating.

Marco's stated purpose in bringing her to his villa was to keep an eye on his mother during his sister's absence, but it was beginning to look as if he had another, and secret, purpose of his own.

It could be that the gate to the beach path was normally padlocked. It could be that Dino had not understood her repeated requests to be taken to the harbour. Maybe she was making a mountain out of a molehill.

It's not that he planned to seduce me, she decided. He's shown no signs of being impressed by my feminine charm. His only interest in my looks is that I'm very like his sister, and—

She caught her breath. *Very like his sister!*

He insisted that she wore Bianca's clothes. Twice, he had asked her to wave to people at a distance— strangers who couldn't possibly know her. He had encouraged her to play Bianca's guitar.

'So!' She spoke aloud, and the lizard flickered into his crack with the speed of lightning. Was that what her host was up to? Had he brought her here to act as a stand-in for his absent sister? It was all right, was it, to be seen driving in the open beach buggy with Dino? But not permitted to stroll around the town where anybody could see she wasn't Bianca Cellini?

So where was Bianca? Was she dead? No, because even an autocrat like Marco could hardly conceal a death for long. Had she eloped, made a marriage of which her brother disapproved? Young Italian girls

45

of good family were strictly brought up and expected to obey the male head of the house, but Bianca's room and her possessions suggested she had absorbed some pretty modern notions. So she might be defying Marco somewhere. Perhaps he had her locked up in some horrible dungeon in the rocks until she submitted and did whatever it was he wanted.

Whatever his motive, he had no right to involve Jan in it, without telling her. The more she thought about it, the more angry she became. She shivered suddenly, and saw that her bare arms had goose-pimpled. Not because she was apprehensive about her own situation, but because the sun had moved and left her in deep shade.

She moved over, following the warmth, stretched full length, prone under the orange trees, her chin on her hands. He couldn't keep me here after the end of my holiday; there's the British Consul, with my passport; and the bank, dealing with my lost travellers' cheques. They know I'm here. The masquerade will have to end when my holiday ends, and Marco knows it.

The scent of orange blossom and canna lilies was heavy this morning, so presently she gathered up her swimming things and went to the pool. There was time for a leisurely swim before her Italian lesson with the Signora.

After the lesson, the walk round the garden with Signora Cellini, the slow walk from one plant to the next. As they passed the white arched gate, Dino greeted them. The boy was washing and polishing the gaily painted buggy, and the sight of the little vehicle put a mischievous idea into Jan's mind.

She left her companion in the long gallery overlooking the sea, and raced back to the gate, snatching up her Greek canvas shoulder-bag as she passed the pool.

'Dino, the Signora wants you at once—in the open gallery, by the bronze statue. Hurry!'

The boy dropped his polishing cloth and ran off on brown bare feet. Jan gave him a couple of minutes' start, then slipped into the driving seat and started the engine. The thing was simplicity itself to drive, but Jan remembered the eight hairpin bends on the precipitous road to the harbour, and went carefully. She had no doubt the Signora would believe she had sent for Dino, and find him a dozen jobs to do among the flowers before releasing him. She had plenty of time.

Parking her vehicle, Jan wandered round the harbour, watching the boats rocking on azure water, the fishermen mending coloured nets; peering into blue-painted wooden pails to admire the striped and gaudy fish so different from any she had seen on an English fishmonger's slab. Pretty, they looked, but she had learned by experience that none had the good flavour of cold-water fish, cod and plaice, halibut and sole.

Leaving the harbour, she soon discovered the town, which had a miniature piazza surrounded by shops and cafés, and with a fine though small church at the top of a sweep of steps. A beggar woman sat on the steps by the church door; children played with a ball, a dog slept in the shade. Barini not having a regular ferry service, it had escaped the tourist invasion so far, and Jan enjoyed the experience of seeing the beauty of the old buildings and shops not swallowed up in advertisements of hotels, restaurants, and garages. There was, however, a bright clean café with basket chairs and coloured umbrellas, and here, when she began to feel hot and tired after her explorations, she sat for a while, ordered a coffee-flavoured ice, and thought about Marco.

Contact with the workaday world of the harbour had blown away her fanciful ideas about Bianca and the dungeon in the rocks. Perhaps even the idea that her host wished her to impersonate his sister to disguise her absence was a bit far-fetched too. She had been unjust to him, though luckily only in her thoughts.

He had rescued her from a nasty situation like a true knight errant; offered her the hospitality of his magnificent villa; given his servant orders to drive her anywhere she wished in his absence. That he had offered her not only his sister's rooms but also her clothes and possessions might, for all she knew, be a form of extravagant Italian hospitality.

Am I annoyed that he did not follow up all this generosity by paying attentions and compliments? Piqued that I failed to attract him?

She paid for her ice-cream and walked on. Until her money arrived, she could buy nothing beyond a few postcards and stamps. The few hundred lire she gathered up from odd pockets and crannies in her hotel room would not go far.

A marquetry shop attracted her. Here were boxes of all sizes, tables, trays, plaques and pictures delicately made in coloured woods, inlaid sometimes with mother-of-pearl. She decided on small caskets for her special friends at the hospital, the prices here being much lower than on the mainland and, she felt sure, the craftsmanship was better. Farther along the cobbled street there was a shop exhibiting work in onyx and marbles white and red, translucent green, creams and browns. A magnificent green onyx horse with mane and tail flying made her gasp with pleasure, but for practical purposes she examined the ash trays, bookends and little gilt boxes with onyx lids.

When at last she tucked her postcards into the Greek shoulder-bag and turned towards the harbour again, she realised she had lingered the whole morning and it was now nearly lunchtime. Island life was so leisurely that one could completely forget that time existed.

Obviously the town must be visited again when she had money, but for the moment one must hurry or be late for lunch. The meal, simple as it was and served outdoors, was nevertheless a formal one. She ran the last few yards to the harbour.

She had a passenger. Marco was sitting in the buggy, stony-faced with anger.

'You!' he exclaimed when he saw her. 'Where is Dino? I've been waiting twenty minutes. We shall be late for lunch.'

'Dino's not here. He—he wasn't expecting you, was he?'

'Certainly he was. I told him I would be here by noon, and he was to meet me. And what happens? I find a car but no Dino. Two more minutes and I'd have driven off without him.'

'I'm surprised you waited so long,' she challenged. Sheer fright had thrown her into an aggressive mood. What had she done?

'Naturally I assumed Dino had been asked to fetch something from the town for my mother, or I wouldn't have waited at all. Why isn't he here? I assume you came down with him.'

'I'm afraid not. I came alone. I'm an experienced driver, *signore*. It was quite safe.'

'Did Dino allow this? Surely he told you I was to be met at noon? Or did you wander round the shops and forget?'

'He didn't tell me and I didn't forget. I took the buggy without his knowledge. It was outside the gate. He'd been cleaning it and left it there. So I just—took it.'

He gave a small, sarcastic bow, a shrug of his elegant shoulders. 'A guest's privilege, of course, but not altogether considerate. One is supposed to ask whether it is convenient, to make off with the only means of getting up and down the hill.'

'I'm sorry. I shouldn't have taken it without asking.'

49

'Please try to be more thoughtful in future. I gave Dino orders to drive you wherever you wished to go. He would have brought you down if you'd asked.'

He moved into the driving seat, indicated she should get in, and drove off.

'But he didn't,' Jan felt she ought to explain what had happened. 'I asked him yesterday, but he drove all round the island taking me everywhere but to the harbour. And I really did need to buy postcards.'

'I thought you hadn't any money.'

'Odd lire from my pockets and a spare purse, no more.'

He said no more, but concentrated on driving up the twisting road. She stole a glance at him, but his face was set in an expression as cold as marble.

Dino came running to meet them when he heard the engine. He was wringing his hands in distress. 'Oh, *signore*,' he wailed. 'Oh, *signore*, I thought some thief had stolen the buggy. I am so sorry, *signore*. I didn't know what to do.'

'You should have walked down, you stupid lazy boy! Then at least you could have told me about the thief and we could have taken a taxi back. If you hadn't been so idle you'd have found our thief yourself, as I did.'

'The Signorina? Oh—'

The look Dino turned to Jan was compounded of surprise, reproach, distress. 'I'm sorry, Dino,' she said gently. 'It is I who am in trouble, not you. I have explained to the Signore that it was not your fault.'

'All right, all right,' Marco said crossly. 'Spare us the apologies; and Dino, stop snivelling! We shall be late for lunch and Mamma will be upset.'

There was no time for a shower. Jan brushed her smooth shoulder-length hair, coaxed it into turning up at the ends. I must look for a photograph of Bianca, she decided. Does she have my dark hair, my grey eyes and arched brows? The nurses say my skin is my best point, fine and clear. In fact—she smiled at herself and leaned forward into the mirror—not to beat about the bush, chum, flawless.

Why do we look alike at a distance? Michael used to say, ' Jan looks like a woman and walks like a princess,' but he's probably saying that to another girl now.

She was scrambling into one of her own dresses when the significance of what she had just thought struck her motionless. She had thought about Michael, remembered he had left her, without that awful sickening pang of agony. For the first time. Was she getting over him?

The Cellinis, mother and son, were waiting for her. She apologised for her lateness and moved to her seat, which Marco drew out for her with his never-failing formal good maners. But he was frowning.

' Why are you not wearing one of my sister's dresses?'

' Is it a rule, *signore*? Surely I am allowed to decide what I wear? It seemed I had already made too free with your family possessions this morning.'

' Go and change.' It was an order.

' But the Signora is waiting.'

' We shall wait. Mamma, Signorina Jan is not quite ready for lunch. We must wait for her.'

The Signora smiled and bent her head graciously in agreement. Fuming with rage, Jan left the table, went to her room feeling like a child in disgrace, and pulled off her dress. Her hands shook as she snatched down one of Bianca's.

At lunch she was too angry to speak. The fresh-caught fish, the strawberries soaked in wine, tasted like nothing. When his mother had withdrawn for her siesta, Marco said:

' I'm sorry, I forgot. I brought our letters from the mainland. It saves time, to collect them. There is one for you.' He laid an envelope on the table and she saw with a leap of her heart that it was in Michael's writing, readdressed from the Rome hotel.

'Thank you, *signore*.'

'We agreed you should call me Marco when we are alone. Please do so.'

'Marco.'

'That's better. You are not sulking because I scolded you?'

'No. I deserved scolding, for running away with your car. It was a stupid thing to do and I have already apologised. But I am very angry indeed at being ordered away from the table like a child, to change my dress. I tried my best not to keep your mother waiting, yet you forced me to do so.'

'That need not happen again, if you will keep your promises.'

She was longing to be alone and open Michael's letter, but Marco had given her an opening she could not miss. 'Marco, what is the purpose of this—this masquerade? Why do you insist I dress up as your sister? You want people to think she is at home, don't you? I'm not prying in matters which don't concern me, but if I'm to play a part in this deception, at least I should be told something about it.'

His mouth whitened. His eyes, looking at her, were hard as pebbles.

'I am a rich man, Jan. My sister has expensive clothes from good dress houses. You are a working girl, you tell me, and I thought you would enjoy the chance to wear such clothes.'

'You—damned little snob! How dare you! Yes, I earn every penny to pay for my clothes. And yes, some of them are bought at a chain store. But I'm not ashamed of them. If you're ashamed of me, you shouldn't have asked me here as a guest. I'd have come as an employee, for the remainder of my holiday, if you'd offered me a job looking after your mother straight out, instead of disguising it as an invitation.'

The tightness went out of his face. He almost smiled. 'Dear me, what fireworks! I'd no idea you could be so temperamental. Almost Italian, if you'll allow me to say so. I assure you, my only crime was to give you some pleasure.'

'Do you think it gives me pleasure to be *ordered* to wear certain clothes? To be driven around the whole island by a servant who knows perfectly well what I really want? You told him to do that, didn't you? Don't let her get too close to other people, or they'll notice she isn't Bianca. Isn't that what you told Dino?'

'Why should I?'

'That's what I'm asking you. Why? There's a gate leading to a path down to what looks like a private beach. It was open yesterday. Today I found it padlocked. Was that because I tried it yesterday and some-one thought I might go down there and be seen?'

'I didn't know about that. Did you actually go through the gate?'

'A few yards only.'

'The path is dangerous. Probably Dino locked it because he feared you might slip and fall. Our guests are our responsibility. The path leads only to our private beach. If you want to go, I will take you.'

'Thank you. I had a longing to swim in the sea, that's all. We have a pool at the hospital. Not as beautiful as yours, and there are no lilies overhanging the water. But the sea—that's quite something.'

'Very well. We'll swim this evening. I shall be ready at five.'

She swallowed. What could one do, with a man like Marco! He made one feel so deflated. She felt like saying *I don't want to go now!* but he would merely point out how childish that was; besides, it was untrue. She did want to go.

53

'At five. That is kind of you, Marco. If you'll excuse me, I'll read my letter now.'

He called her back. 'Also I should tell you, your passport is ready, and new travel documents. I telephoned the Consul's office. I also enquired at the bank. Your money should be there tomorrow. If I do not need the boat, Dino can take you all the way to Naples. Otherwise, I will take you as far as Ischia and you can catch the ferry from there. If you will not consider me too much of a little snob, I will lend you the money to finance your trip, and you can pay me back when you return in the evening.'

'You took all that trouble for my affairs, when you had business of your own? Marco, I shouldn't have called you a snob, but you just made me so angry I couldn't help myself. You're lucky it wasn't something worse.'

'Don't apologise, my dear Jan. You look lovelier than ever when you are angry, and we Italians enjoy watching a woman in a passion. A touch of hot ginger in a dish lends added pleasure.'

Francesca arrived to clear the luncheon table and seemed confused to find them still there. She made to go away, but Marco called her back, saying he and the Signorina were going.

'You to your siesta, Jan. And I to my work. We shall meet again at five.'

Michael wanted her. The letter was a despairing cry from the heart, but it left Jan cold.

So the other girl had let him down. Just as he had let Jan down. She hadn't wailed for sympathy, and all the tears she had shed had been in private. But this—! She shrugged helplessly. It was just a load of self-pity, which even a month ago would have fooled her, sent her running to poor Michael with little cries of sympathy. Not now.

54

Sorry, Michael, she said as she tore the letter into narrow strips and dropped them in the wastepaper basket. Seems like you're going to have to do some growing up, boy. But not at my expense, thank you.

The louvred shutters were closed against the afternoon sun; the room was cool and dark, smelling of flowers. As Jan drifted into a light sleep, the thought came to her that she had grown out of Michael because she'd met a real man now. The thought must have amused her, for she slept with a little smile on her lips.

She woke with a feeling that something pleasant was about to happen, and lay idly watching the narrow slits of sunlight on the closed shutters. She felt relaxed and rested, the sharp skirmish with Marco half forgotten. In this lotus-land, nothing was important enough to quarrel about. Especially with Marco, who could be so kind when he chose, and even at his worst, never failed in his princely good manners.

Remembering Marco, she remembered they had a date at five o'clock to go swimming. And before that, there would be the Signora Cellini's tea, served on the terrace overlooking the Bay, as delicate and formal as a ballet, with Francesca in a clean white cotton apron and wearing white silk gloves. To-day Marco would be there. Punctilious in his attendance on his mamma, he would never miss her tea-time when on the island.

Jan got up, showered, and pinned her hair into a neat bun on top of her head. It was cooler that way, and would be easier to handle after the sea-water swim. Then she pulled out all Bianca's swim suits and made a careful choice. Italian fashion house or British chain store made little difference when one got down to basic girl-in-a-bikini, and Jan had confidence in her long shapely legs and slim bare midriff. It was the teatime cover-up that was important. She chose a strawberry-red and white polka-dot halter-neck playsuit, with matching choker necklace and lime-green leather sandals. Marco was so right, for the wrong reasons. Good clothes did a lot for a girl's morale.

Marco Cellini had, it seemed, completely forgotten the brush they'd had at lunch, and forgiven her for her theft of the morning. He rose when Jan appeared, kissed her hand and adjusted the big rose-pink fringed umbrella which shaded the white wrought-iron table.

'About Capri,' he began as if they were in the middle of a conversation. 'You cannot leave the Bay of Naples without going there. In spite of the tourism boom, it is still a heavenly spot and I promised to take you. If I am free, we shall go there the day after to-morrow. Tomorrow, you are to collect your valuables in Rome. I have business in Rome, so you must be ready to leave at eight in the morning. We shall travel together, in my car. It will be pleasanter for you than the train.'

'You change your mind quickly, Signor Marco. At lunch you promised to lend me the fare. I can manage alone, truly I can. You're a busy man and I do not wish to be a nuisance.'

'I have changed my mind,' he replied in a tone which forbade argument.

He had changed for the bathe. He wore a white shortie bathrobe, with short sleeves, and was more powerfully built than appeared when formally dressed. Muscular forearms, and legs, were brown as mahogany. His feet, thrust into well-used leather sandals, were shapely and strong. As he conversed with his mother, Jan studied him with professional interest; the muscles beneath the satin smooth skin, the bone beneath the muscles. Almost one could take him for the original model of some of those old Roman gods, bronze or marble, in the museums and gardens she had seen.

'Well,' he said at last, with a smile in her direction

which would have set any woman's pulse stirring, ' shall we go? You need reliable sandals on your feet, not those nonsensical ankle-twisters you're wearing. Put on the pair you were wearing this morning. We have a lot of clambering to do, and I promise you I'm not prepared to carry you up the cliff if you damage yourself.'

She said demurely, ' The ankle-twisters belong to your sister. The reliable ones are my own.'

He acknowledged the shaft with a rueful grin. ' Touché! You have a quick tongue. I wouldn't care to trust you with a rapier.'

Without a word, Jan unrolled her scarlet towel. The approved sandals were rolled in it. Did he think her such a fool as to attempt the cliff steps in fashion sandals?

His eyebrows rose in surprise, mock or genuine. ' Mamma, this is the first young woman who ever got the better of me, and made me laugh at myself! '

' Your father said the same thing about me. It is good for a man to have to laugh at himself sometimes. Otherwise he becomes pompous. Your father was never pompous.'

Marco glanced quickly at Jan, meeting her eyes in a question. The Signora had spoken of her husband in the past tense. Jan's Italian grammar being shaky, she had not been quite sure until she saw Marco's reaction.

' You are doing my mother good,' he said as they started the climb down to the beach. ' I wish you would stay with her as a companion. I will double whatever they pay you at your hospital.'

' I need notice of that question. How can I decide such an important step while hanging on to a cliffside by my eyebrows?'

' You'll think about it?'

' Who wouldn't? A fat salary, an easy patient, the

57

Bay of Naples. I'll think about, it, Marco. But don't be too hopeful. I'm too young to get myself trapped in a cul-de-sac and say goodbye to all ambition.'

The path led down between banks of flowers whose warm scent filled the air. Broom there was, in golden cascades, and herb-scented shrubby plants, and great clumps of moon-daisies. Though the going was steep, the steps were well kept and there were good hand-holds. When Marco called a halt for a rest, it was possible to see a thumbnail-shaped bay between two headlands, which could only be reached by water.

'Can't one walk round at low tide?' Jan wondered.

'There is no tide in the Tyrrhenian sea, you ignorant girl!'

'Sorry, I forgot. Could one swim round?'

'Only if one were an exceptionally good swimmer. The cliffs go sheer into the sea on either side, and there would be no place to moor a boat.'

Jan pointed below them. 'How do we manage the last bit? From here, it looks as if the cliff ends in mid-air over a sheer drop.'

He chuckled. 'It does. The last part of the descent is by ladder.'

'Help!'

'An iron one, cemented into the rock. We keep it in repair, though no one uses the beach nowadays. I used to, as a boy, but Bianca complains the climb up again spoils the cooling effect of the swim.'

'Why isn't it overgrown, if no one uses it?'

'What an inquisitive girl you are! I've no idea. Probably Dino or one of the men about the place clears it from time to time. They may use it for swimming, for all I know.'

'I see. You did give Dino orders to lock it, didn't you?'

'No. He misunderstood me. I told him not to allow

you to get yourself lost, and to keep an eye on you. He exceeded his orders, that's all.'

'Then it was for his own reasons he didn't want me down here.'

Marco gave her a sharp glance. 'What makes you say that?'

'I wonder about things, that's all. The hinge on the gate was oiled.'

'I have an efficient staff. Shall we move on, or do you want to rest a few moments longer?'

'On. I can't wait to get into the sea. Blue, emerald, turquoise, green, azure. It fascinates me. Is it warm?'

The ladder was vertical, the descent longer than Jan had imagined. Looking down, she felt slightly sick. It would be awful to fail now, but she wished heartily she had not been so insistent upon coming down to the sea.

'There's always a first time,' Marco smiled. 'Once you've done it, you won't think a thing about it. Wait, now.' He went down several rungs, then leaned outward, his arms outstretched as he gripped the sides of the ladder firmly. 'Come down to me. Don't look down, I'll tell you when to stop. Put your feet into the rungs, please, not on my face.' She felt his hand take a grip of her heel and guide her foot. 'That's right. Now I am holding you, you cannot fall. Move when I move. Left foot down now.'

She was all but clasped in his arms as they moved down step by step. All she could see were the iron steps, the riven and striated rock, the outcrop of tiny flowering plants. She could feel the warmth of his body close to hers, hear his breathing.

'Are you all right, Jan?'

'Yes, thank you. I feel perfectly safe.'

'In my arms?' She heard him chuckle quietly. The wretch, he was mocking her very natural fears.

Would she ever understand this man, with his

lightning changes of mood?

Feet on the hot sand at last, Jan craned her neck to see the route they had travelled. 'I'll do it alone next time. I don't intend to let a silly old ladder get the better of me.' Eager for the pleasure of the salt water, she stepped out of the playsuit, revealing a hot red silk jersey bikini with shoestring straps which she had chosen to set off her creamy skin.

Marco tilted back his head and looked at her through half-closed eyes. 'Clever girl! On Bianca it is a failure. Why?'

'Possibly because she swims in the Mediterranean sun more often than I can. Is she tanned?'

He snapped his fingers. 'That's it. We almost never see a true milk-white skin. Jan, you are really beautiful.'

She laughed happily. 'You've made my day! With a newly mended heart to my credit, a smashing compliment was just what I needed, like cream on strawberries.'

'Tell me about this heart of yours? Was it broken?'

'In a thousand pieces. I almost died. Then one day I looked and it wasn't even cracked.'

'You hadn't loved him after all.'

She thought a minute, shifting the sand with her toe. 'Oh yes, Marco—I loved him.'

'But you found someone you loved more, perhaps?'

'Now who's inquisitive? No, funnily enough, it wasn't that. I just realised one day that he wasn't grown up and probably never would be. Or not till he stopped loving himself more than anybody else.'

'Was he handsome?'

She narrowed her eyes, trying to recall all the details of Michael's face she knew so well, with her eyes, her hands, her mouth.

'I don't think so. His face just added up to— Michael. Looks don't matter, except at the very beginning. Once you're in love you only see the one person shining through.'

'You think you may love again?'

'Goodness, I hope so. I'm twenty-one. I'd hate to think my love life was ended.'

'It won't be. I see strings of beautiful young men in your future.'

'One will be enough, if he's the right one.'

He reached out both hands, cupped her smooth shoulders and pulled her towards him. His mouth came down hard on hers. This was a man's kiss, insistent, demanding, confident.

Her body, unprepared, leapt to respond. She felt an overwhelming urge to grasp, to clutch, to yield. But as his arms and mouth pressed more insistently, she recoiled, rigid in his arms, and made a desperate effort to turn away her face. When he became aware of her resistance, he released her so abruptly that she staggered, almost lost her balance. He steadied her with a cool strong hand on her waist.

'Why did you do that?' she flung at him. 'Kissing wasn't in our bargain.'

'You bargain for kisses?' he asked lightly, a mocking smile on his lips. 'I think you owed me that one. Now you know how a grown-up man kisses, and experience is always valuable, is it not?'

He turned and raced towards the water.

Aware of the inner excitement his kiss had roused in her, aware that here was a powerful and dangerous man accustomed to having his own way completely in his own domain, she hesitated only a moment before following. They had come down here to swim, and swim they must, if the situation was to be brought back to the level of their normal relationship. She was no child, to make a fuss about a single kiss. Accept it and forget it was the best course to adopt. An amorous, temporary affair with her host was the last thing she

61

wanted; nor did she intend to spend the rest of her stay at the Villa Tramonti dodging a man who was physically attracted to her.

She made a long running dive, and when she came up and shook the water off her face, he was close by, watching. He grinned and shouted as if nothing had happened.

' How do you like the Tyrrhenian Sea?'

' Great!' she laughed.

He dived and swam under water. In the clear emerald sea, bubbles of air enveloped his body, so she could see him, a silver man, swimming below her over the silver sand.

They swam, or floated lazily, until Marco called to her that he was going out. She followed him up the beach and flopped down beside him on the spread towels.

' That was absolutely wonderful! Oh, Marco, bless you—a cigarette.' She leaned over to take a light from his cupped hands. ' Just perfect! Have we time to sunbathe?'

' Until we run out of sun. We shall lose it round the headland soon.' He lay on his back, fingers linked behind his head. ' Tell me about yourself. Are you going to accept my offer of a job here with us?'

She shook her head. ' Uh-huh!'

' Uh-huh yes, or uh-huh no?'

' No. I'd like to. I want to—at this moment. But I've worked three hard years for my finals and I intend to sit them. Then I'll be qualified, and be something. A properly qualified nurse, with experience, can work almost anywhere she pleases, do you know that? Australian outback, Canada, the Arctic— you name it, people get sick and want nursing. Besides—' She hesitated, drawing a line in the sand with her finger.

' Besides—?' he queried, craning up to look at her.

' I am a *valuable* person, as a nurse. I can nurse

genuinely sick people, people who need me. Your mother doesn't need a nurse. She needs something to do. Someone to talk to. It may be her choice or yours that she lives like an elegant cabbage, but you shouldn't allow her to fold her hands and opt out of life just because your father died.'

'They did everything together—everything.'

'So you should be encouraging her to continue with what they started. One must have some purpose in life, and—well, it seems to me that if one is taken and the other left, there's a purpose behind it. There's something left to be done. Marco, your mother could die of sheer boredom perched up on the top of your island. But she is not ill, and she doesn't need a nurse.'

'I have a good apartment in Rome, but she hates the city. Any suggestions, while you're busy reorganising my life for me?'

'I have. But you'd be angry with me. You are not a patient man, Marco Cellini.'

'Pretend I am.'

She gave him a long, steady look. 'You asked for it, Marco. All right. When Dino took me all around the island pretending he didn't know I wanted the the harbour, I saw a lot of poverty. Too much. Some appalling housing, only habitable because of your wonderful climate. Some crippled children. Some beggars. *Beggars*, Marco! To me, that is unthinkable. Little kids, begging in the road! You say you own a good deal of Barini—you and your father before you. Don't you feel any sort of responsibility for the people, for the way they live?'

'We've done a good deal, in our time. You're not suggesting my *mother* took some responsibility for houses and layabouts who won't work to keep their children?'

'I wouldn't dare suggest anything to Barini's lord and master. All I'm saying is that there is much to be done, or left undone, by someone.'

'I see.' The coldness edged into his voice again. 'Well, now you've demonstrated that I'm an incompetent landlord, a wicked son, is there anything else you'd like to sharpen your stiletto on while you're making it so obvious you hate the sight of me?'

'I'm not too sure of your performance as a brother, either. But I don't hate the sight of you. You're extremely decorative lying there on the sand, like one of your own gorgeous statues—alive, but with a stone heart perhaps. I wish I understood you, Marco. So far, you've shown yourself a lion, a tiger, a bear, a— ow!'

He had swung over and grabbed her ankle in a steel grip.

'Don't torment the wild animals, girl. Just—wait— till—I—get—a grip—'

Aware that she had gone too far, and could hardly hope to escape Marco's vengeance now, she lashed out with her captured leg, kicking him fair and square in the chest. While he gasped to recover the breath she had knocked out of him, she scrambled to her feet and flew barefooted across the sand to the ladder, began to climb rung over rung at top speed. The steepness and height were forgotten now.

A lion, a tiger, a bear. Yes, he was all of those. But what she had foolishly overlooked in her baiting of him was that Marco Cellini was also a man. And such men are dangerous.

At the top of the ladder, she paused, gasping for breath, and glanced down. He had stopped to put on his sandals. Prudent Marco! Had he done that to protect his feet, or was he genuinely unwilling to catch her?

No, he was really coming after her. He belted his towelling wrap tightly, then started across the sand. Wise, then. In sandals he would make better speed on the rock staircase. She began to climb again, pulling herself up by clumps of shrub, taking risks as she leapt from narrow stair to narrow stair. When she reached the top and came out through the gate to the level terrace, her feet were scratched, bleeding, and bruised. But Marco was still coming up fast and she dared not stop.

She raced across the garden, swung round the pool, took a flying jump across a bed of rare ferns. The long louvres which kept Bianca's room cool through the long hot days were closed. Her fingers scrabbled at the fastening. Then she was through, as Marco leapt over the ferns, taking the same short cut as she had used but a minute before.

Across the sitting room and into the bedroom, slamming the door shut. Surely he would not pursue her into here? While she still clung, panting, to the long curved satin-brass handle, something went thump! on the door.

Silence! Eaten with curiosity to know what Marco had thrown, she opened the door a crack and peered out. Her sandal. She squatted on her heels, reached out a cautious hand to draw it in, when *thump!* came the second one.

Then there really was silence. Jan waited a long time, till her heart stopped thudding and she began to shiver in the cool room. Then she opened the door. The sitting room was empty, the louvres shut. But her second sandal lay pathetically upside down in a little sandy patch on the shining white marble floor.

She showered, and rinsed the salt out of her hair, then pinned it into place and blew it dry with Bianca's drier.

Of one thing she could be sure. Lion, tiger, or bear; or an angry man bent on vengeance, Marco Cellini would appear at his mother's dinner table suave, charming, exquisitely dressed and perfectly mannered.

So tonight she would wear the most beautiful dress in his sister's wardrobe. Just to show him that two could play at that game!

CHAPTER IV

On the journey to Rome, Marco was taciturn. Jan had the impression that his silence had nothing to do with the events of the previous day. He was preoccupied with his own affairs. Last night after dinner he had excused himself immediately with a plea of work to do and telephone calls to make, and had not reappeared.

He took the fast motorway route from Naples to Rome. The flowering broom and acacia made the road a river of gold and perfume.

'Thank you for bringing me,' she said when Marco had parked and switched off the engine. 'You've saved me hours of travelling. I don't want to be a nuisance, as I know you have business in Rome. I'll manage fine on my own. Here, at least, I know my way about.'

There had been no difficulty in finding parking space. Like everyone else, he had parked on the sidewalk. 'If you *knew your way about*, as you put it, you'd never have met me or come to Barini. I shall accompany you to the bank, but first you will need your passport and travel documents. Come along.'

Keeping up with his long strides was not easy when one had to dodge in and out of the racing traffic. Jan felt like a pet poodle on the end of a lead. Marco never looked back to see if she was following, taking it for granted that she would be at his heels when he stopped. Twice her heart was in her mouth as he swung confidently out to cross a road, marching straight into the traffic with arm upraised like an ancient Roman senator. She recalled with rueful amusement her own efforts to cross the controlled pedestrian walks, her fury when drivers did not slow down but merely twisted round her as if she had no right to be on the crossing at all.

'The important thing,' Marco said when at last he stopped and waited for her to catch up, 'is never to lose your nerve. Hold up your arm and march. Never dither. What are you going to do with yourself for the rest of the day? I shall be free at four-thirty.'

'One last day in Rome? Of course, it must be the Vatican. I want to go up on the roof of St Peter's to see the view, and I believe it's possible to walk inside the dome and look down into the basilica.'

'It is. See the treasury too. Tourists often miss that, as it opens only at special hours. There's a board giving the times, in the church. There you'll see the the finest work of gold and silver craftsmen for centuries past; all the greatest artists in the world have worked for the Holy City. There are gifts from countries, cities, kings and princes, popes and cardinals; the best their countries could produce, from the earliest centuries to—to, let me see—Winston Churchill and President Kennedy.'

'That I must see. Then I want to walk along the Via Veneto, and I thought I could lunch there, out of doors, if it wouldn't be too expensive.'

He smiled. 'Said to be the most elegant and beautiful street in the world. Or, shall we say, one of them? You'd be happier with a male escort, I think. I shall take you there, at one o'clock.'

'Oh, but I didn't mean—I wasn't hinting, Marco.'

'I know. After yesterday, you are just a little afraid of me, aren't you? You need not be. I am not a seducer of innocent maidens, in spite of your thinking me a bear, a lion, and a tiger. Let me see—we must be quite sure of our meeting place. Be waiting by the obelisk in the centre of the colonnade in St Peter's Square at twelve-forty-five precisely. I will pick you up there.'

Demurely, she said, 'Yes, *signore*.' He caught the

twinkle in her eyes as she spoke.

'You think I am a dictator, yes? But I merely wish to make sure there is no mistake as to the place and time. I never keep a lady waiting, and in a big and busy city like Rome, it is not a good thing for a driver to be kept waiting. Your training as a nurse should make you appreciate the virtues of precision.'

'It does. I shall be there.' The hours she'd wasted waiting for Michael, the reproaches she had swallowed. His righteous, innocent indignation when she had not been able to keep back a grumble. He never understood that time could matter.

The formalities did not take long.

'How good it feels to have possessions again! This is Bianca's handbag, so the first thing I'm going to do is to buy one for myself. And some of my own make-up, and a decent comb. If I won a jackpot I couldn't be more delighted.'

Marco reached over and took the little wad of travellers' cheques out of her hand. 'You can have that one. I'll keep the rest. And give me your passport and tickets, please.'

Suspicions she had succeeded in burying leapt to the forefront of her mind. What was he up to? Without money, tickets, passport, she was at his mercy. Part of the relief she felt at having them back was the knowledge that she was independent again; could move about, when and where she liked. She would be foolish indeed to surrender everything but pocket money for the day, into this man's hands. He was, after all, a stranger. One girl he said was his sister had disappeared from his house.

She drew back sharply. 'No, thank you. I'd like to keep everything. It's so wonderful to have it all back again. Like a miracle. I hardly believed it would come. So if you don't mind—'

He kept his hand extended. 'All right, keep some

69

more for your shopping. But I can't guarantee a rescuer appearing for the second time, and you didn't manage very well on the earlier occasion, did you? You need that money and other things, for getting home. So let me keep them in my briefcase where they'll be safe. No bag-snatcher will have a chance to grab them from *me*.'

Common sense. He talked common sense all the time. He made it sound so plausible. Yet the plain fact was that once she parted with her passport, she'd be his prisoner again.

'Hurry,' he said crisply. 'We haven't all morning to waste. You've planned a programme for yourself you won't accomplish in a whole day as it is. Take a taxi to the Vatican. Be sure he has his meter operating and don't give more than ten per cent tip.'

What could she do? Go back into the bank and claim that her elegant young escort was trying to rob her? A rich, well-known businessman? She might make a run for it, and finish off her holiday in the hotel room for which she'd paid. But if he chose, he could then make things difficult for her. She was clad from head to foot in his sister's clothes, and carrying an expensive handbag which wasn't hers.

She surrendered the items he'd asked for. 'What happens if I meet your sister in Rome, and she has me arrested for theft?'

His eyebrows lifted. Devil's eyebrows, pointed rather than curved.

'Bianca in Rome? I hardly think so. You know she is in Florence, visiting her aunt. Still, if you're nervous—' He took a business card from his wallet, scribbled a word or two across the back. 'If you meet with any trouble, use this.' He laughed abruptly. 'I'll warrant it would bring Bianca to her senses!'

So Bianca needed bringing to her senses, did she? And Marco, for all his confidence, thought it possible she might turn up in Rome? Racing headlong towards St Peter's in the taxi Marco had hailed for her, Jan turned the idea over in her mind. She felt a sympathy, almost an affection, for the girl. Young and filled with modern ideas of independence and freedom, she would undoubtedly find the slow, even tenor of the long days at the Villa Tramonti boring beyond endurance. One would need to be deeply in love, and fully involved with the life of the island, to live there permanently. So it was likely Bianca had run away. Eloped, maybe, with the boy of her choice. And Marco hadn't a clue to her whereabouts.

Jan chuckled to herself. If that were the truth, it served Marco Cellini jolly well right!

Just then her taxi-driver decided to race two others to get through the narrowing gap between two converging buses, and Jan closed her eyes waiting for the crash. When nothing happened except a great deal of shrieked abuse, she opened them cautiously again, and found she had already arrived between the great stone wings of Bernini's magnificent colonnade, with St Peter's church in front of her.

Going up in the lift, she found herself on a flat roof from which she had all-embracing views of the city of Rome, the river Tiber, the gardens of the Vatican. The stone statues of Christ and his apostles which dominated St Peter's Square and seemed, from ground level, a little larger than life-size, were now revealed as giants. Tourists and photographers, gazing in awe at close quarters, were pygmies. How strange it seemed, she thought as she gazed over the parapet at the toy traffic below, the insect-humans moving to and fro, that centuries ago, when the magnificent Roman Forum now in ruins was in its heyday, this very spot, now so revered, was the cruel Roman circus. Under this same sky, this same blazing sun, thousands of young Christians had been martyred by those Romans, and buried where they fell. Ordinary people, common people, who worked and paid taxes and got tired and frightened, their lives ending in a mess of blood and stink, dust and terror, because they had enough courage to die for what they knew.

How could they have imagined such a vast and splendid monument over their poor crushed bones and mangled bodies? Or dreamed that one day the whole world would come, day after day, to visit their splendid tomb and stare at the broken remnants of the empire which swatted them down like flies? A girl my age, in love with life and maybe with a boy in chains beside her, hearing the lions roar and smelling the foetid odour of the wild-animal cages? Would it have comforted them, to see all the people coming and going, drawn from countries undiscovered then, to this vast magnet?

Time had flown. There was just enough for her to climb in ever-narrowing circles up inside the dome to the topmost gallery and see an even wider view of the city and the hills on which it had been built. The city on seven hills! On the way down, she went inside the dome and stared into the body of the great basilica, the top of the baldaquin over the High Altar.

Then it was time to hurry down to the obelisk where Marco would arrive prompt on his hour. To her relief, she was there first, looking out for his low white car.

He arrived, after all, in a horse-drawn open *botticella* which sported a bright new flowered canopy with a deep white fringe, and fresh clean covers of the same material over the seats. The coachwork shone, the horse was well-groomed and in good condition. Trust Marco to find such a splendid vehicle out of all the tatty carriages, all the bone-tired thin horses in the city.

' In you get,' he smiled, and handed her in with a flourish, touching her hand to his lips as he did so. ' I said you needed an escort for the most elegant street in Europe, and it occurred to me you needed a carriage too.'

Almost too astonished to answer, she gave him a brilliant smile of thanks and seated herself, feeling like a queen going to her coronation. The horse travelled at a spanking trot down the broad processional way of the Via della Conciliazione.

He laid a hand on hers. 'Happy, Jan?'

'Over the moon with sheer joy. I can't even thank you, Marco. How could you think of such a lovely thing, when you're so busy with your own affairs? You really are a most remarkable person.'

'So are you—young, lovely, with all the world before you. Yet you plan such a hardworking, unglamorous life for yourself. Don't you want any fun, any luxury, any—love?'

'I want all those things. I'm not such a fool as to think they make up the whole of life. Fun and luxury only exist for those who rarely get them. Have them all the time and they are commonplace.'

'You open new vistas on the feminine mind, *signorina*. What are your astonishing views on marriage, if one may ask?'

'A partnership. A sharing. Love—I don't know. Perhaps it's different for everybody, but for me it must go a long way beyond the physical. There must be tenderness, and caring, and a sort of astonishment and delight.'

'Does it last?'

'How should I know? Your parents' love lasted, didn't it? I have an idea that if love was real, one might never get to the end of it, but always be discovering new marvels right to the end of time.'

'You're an idealist. But in your country you believe in marriage for love.'

'And yours are arranged, are they not?'

73

'Quite often. Especially in the older, more traditional families. Often big estates are involved, vast businesses or fortunes. It would not do, you see, to trust to love. One also needs common sense, and common sense is not a noticeable feature of lovers.'

'I think that is quite dreadful! Love can't be arranged.'

'It often is. The majority of such marriages are successful. Can you say your own system has a higher proportion of successes than ours? Can two youngsters crazily in love see the pitfalls?'

'Often. But foolishly believe love will carry them safely over. Sometimes it does, too. Are you in love, Marco? I'm not prying, I just meant are you officially betrothed and looking forward to a happy marriage?'

'No, I'm not. Eligible daughters are constantly paraded before me, of course. That's inevitable. But they're all so—' he shrugged and spread his hands in an expressive gesture, 'predictable. Educated at the same schools, reared in the same atmosphere, dressed in the same fashions—'

'Is Bianca like that?'

'I don't know. I'm her brother. She's just a child— no, that's not true. She is a really lovely girl and, I suppose, ripe for marriage. When she comes home, I shall suggest to her fiancé that he puts the wedding forward. I had asked him to wait a year as she is so young.'

She cried in surprise, 'Bianca's *engaged*! You never told me!'

'My dear, do you think I would neglect my duty to a sister? Certainly I have found her a good marriage. He is young, rich, has a fine estate in Tuscany. Bianca will be a *contessa*.'

'Great! If she wants to be. Does she love him?'

'Love comes after marriage, our women admit that. You look doubtful, but if love can die after marriage,

74

can it not also be born?'

'Y-yes, I should think so. But how awful, if it didn't, and one had to face a lifetime with a man one didn't love.'

'You have other plans for yourself, eh? A lifetime of service to the sick and old.'

'How dull you make my career sound. I assure you, if and when I meet the right man, I shall be happy to marry and have a home and children of my own. Only I happen to think that domestic duties are not enough to occupy one's whole time. I'd probably be a better wife for having interests outside the house. I'd stay younger and be a more complete person, so perhaps I'd be more attractive and interesting to my husband and other people. A cabbage existence I couldn't abide.'

The little carriage had now begun to encounter the heavy motor traffic in the narrower streets, and progress was slower. Marco made the driver stop once or twice, so that Jan could admire the huge fountains with their enormous figures spouting water in innumerable cascades. And at last they entered the Via Veneto by the Pincine Gate, and Jan reluctantly said goodbye to the shining *botticella*.

They ate outside, under a striped pink and white awning. The smart tables were covered in deep pink linen cloths, and banked with flowers.

'I shall choose everything for you,' Marco said at once. 'Including the wine, for how can you possibly know what is best for such an occasion?'

During lunch he proved a delightful companion, knowledgeable and witty. Please don't let me fall in love with him, Jan prayed, for if I do I'll never recover, and never find anyone so charming, when he exerts himself to be; so masterful and confident, so difficult to understand completely. One would never get to the end of making discoveries about him, she thought. He can make a woman feel like a queen or a beggarmaid, and be sublimely unaware that he was doing either.

And when he kissed, he could make a girl feel like a woman. Even now, as exquisitely dressed women and deft waiters moved between the tables, among the scent of massed flowering plants and shrubs, the noise of the Rome traffic and the glimpse of a tall palm tree reflected in the plate glass window of the hotel, the memory of his hard male kiss could stir her. Would it ever be repeated?

Better, safer, not. Her best chance was to get back to England and her examinations, and forget the Rome episode.

At last he glanced at his watch. 'Alas, I must go. Work calls. Where for you?'

'I didn't have time to see the treasury or do my shopping.'

'You can shop anywhere. Do that in Capri. Nowhere else in the world can you see the jewels of the Vatican—rubies, emeralds, diamonds, pearls. Crowns and crucifixes, cloth-of-gold robes and jewelled Orders—'

'Wouldn't it be better to sell all that, and give the money to the poor?'

'Who could buy? They are beyond price. And if some millionaire bought even a fraction of what has been given with such love and faith over so many ages —wouldn't people still be saying the same thing, in *his* country? Man is not forbidden to give glory to God, and still take care of the poor and sick. One Michelangelo for the glory, one Jan to nurse the sick. Both have their place. Off you go, now. No *botticella* next time. It will be the car and straight back to Naples, where we will dine. Don't be late, mind.'

It was midnight before they arrived at the Villa Tramonti. Signora Cellini had waited up for them, and came hurrying through the garden to meet them.

'Have you brought Bianca?' she called anxiously. 'You are so late, both of you. Bianca, my love, you should not have allowed your brother to keep you out till midnight. It is not discreet for a young lady. And you will miss your beauty sleep.'

'I am not Bianca, madame,' Jan said gently. 'See— I'm Jan. Bianca is in Florence with her aunt.'

Marco put a tender arm round his mother's shoulders. 'Mamma, you must not begrudge the child a little holiday. She is having a fine time with her aunt and cousins.'

The Signora stared at him hardly, not a sign of confusion in her handsome face. 'Then why doesn't she write? Why, why, why?'

Jan's heart turned over. At last Marco would have to say something definite.

He turned towards the wide open doors of the villa, drawing his mother with him. 'She did write, darling. Don't you remember? She told us all about her visit to the Uffizi Galleries, and Aunt Tina's liver trouble.'

'Never, never! You're lying, Marco. You lie all the time. My daughter is dead, isn't she? Like my husband.'

'Mamma, I've told you a hundred times, Bianca is nothing of the sort. She's as strong and well as I am. Don't cry, please don't cry, little Mamma!'

The Signora was sobbing, beyond her control. She buried her face in her hands and shook with crying. 'Liar, liar, liar!'

Marco, murmuring gently, tried to draw her hands from her face. Without warning, his mother flung up her head, and screaming *Liar!* once more, struck him heavily across the cheek.

Quicker than thought, Jan scooped water from the fountain in her cupped palms and dashed it into the older woman's face. The Signora gasped and shivered.

'Hysteria!' Jan snapped over her shoulder to Marco. 'Leave her to me. This is my job.'

Gently she led the trembling woman indoors, helped her to undress and put her to bed. There were sleeping tablets in a small onyx box by the bedside, so Jan administered one and put the box out of reach. Then she closed the shutters and sat quietly waiting till the sobs died down and more even breathing told her the Signora slept.

Then she went outside. Marco was slumped in a chair by the fountain, staring at nothing. She sat on the marble lip of the *terrazzo*. After a minute she said:

'Start talking, Marco. You'll have to tell me now, won't you? Where is your sister?'

He gave a heavy sigh, then lifted his head and spoke. 'I haven't the slightest idea.'

'You don't *know*? Your sister disappears and you do nothing but calmly import a strange girl who happens to look a bit like her? Where do you *think* she is?'

He twisted towards her, with an expression of murderous rage. 'For God's sake, woman, shut up!'

Jan compressed her lips, got up and marched into her bedroom, where she stripped off every last stitch of Bianca's outfit, rolled it into a ball. Then she put on her own simple skirt and cotton sweater, and went back into the garden. Marco was there. He was holding a cigarette between his fingers now, the smoke rising in a thin line of blue under the *terrazzo* lantern.

'Enough is enough, Marco. Either you tell me exactly what you know about your sister here and now, or I quit. The masquerade is finished. Do you understand? Are you listening?'

'Don't shout. There's nothing I can tell, you silly little fool.'

'Right. Goodbye. I'm going to pack now and I

shall leave first thing in the morning.' She threw the bundle of Bianca's clothes at him. Hard driven by temper, it hit him on the head and rolled down his shoulders, unfolding as it went.

Jan swung on her heel and marched indoors, banging the louvres after her. Hands shaking with rage, she dragged out her suitcase and began to thrust her things in. She could get back to the Rome hotel now she had her money. The room there was paid for, till Saturday.

Saturday! She stopped, struck by the thought that she was due back in England at the end of this week.

There's to be no more. Nothing. No Marco ever again!

And she loved him.

Love? Was that possible, after so short an acquaintance? Didn't the kind of love she craved grow gently, come into flower slowly; a wondrous thing of the mind and spirit, as well as of the body and the beating pulses? How much of what she had felt for Michael had been real love, and how much the simple magnetism of young body to young body, the leap of the stirred blood, the eternal male-female pull?

But Michael had been a boy. Marco was an intensely masculine man, with all the masculine qualities of leadership and confidence. He was autocratic in a country where men were expected to be autocratic, to be the heads of their families, to rule and be obeyed. He was dependable, thoughtful in small ways as well as great. He was the head of big business, a man of wealth; and how could he have achieved that, without being tough, determined, strong?

But emotionally? What did she know about him emotionally? Unlike most of his fellow-countrymen, who wore their emotions like banners, Marco kept his feelings under stern control. There could be a volcano under that stern crust, but only an occasional shower of white-hot sparks hinted at the locked-in fires.

With an uncontrollable desire to escape from her racing thoughts, she pushed open the shutters which led to the balcony of Bianca's bedroom, and stepped out. The sky was velvet black and studded with stars. The flower scents of the day rose powerfully on the cooling air. Somewhere out there, hidden in the dark, was Vesuvius, that sleeping giant—dead, some believed, since the eruption of 1944. Was it extinct? Or merely biding its time again?

This was the end. The end of her holiday, which had started so modestly, and become so unexpectedly luxurious. Which had started with tears for lost Michael, and would end with tears for lost Marco Cellini.

How stupid could one get? She clenched her fists on the white-painted wrought-iron balcony, angry with herself. She had tumbled headlong into the love-trap again, after escaping once with a whole skin and even a whole heart. What a fool!

After the long hot day, she should have been tired and ready for bed. But she felt full of a restless vitality. The sharp scene with the Cellinis, mother and son, had driven sleep from her brain. She was wondering whether the coast would be clear for her to steal out to the swimming pool, when the remembrance of Signora Cellini brought her up sharply.

She slipped a linen jacket over her bare arms, kicked off her sandals and pushed her feet into soft slippers, then stole silently out into the garden, on her way to the Signora's bedroom. Although she had seen the Signora safetly in bed and asleep only a short time ago, the older woman was disturbed and distressed, frail in spite of her quiet life and the modest activities in the garden. It was high time Jan took a peep at her patient.

The garden was empty. The white chairs were

grouped around the table as if for a tea-party of ghosts. From this side of the house one could see the sea far below, a broad white pathway painted across it by a full moon riding serenely on high like a polished dinner-plate. The moon, the scented lilies, the white furniture—and nothing more but the deep blue of sky and sea, the dark shadows, silence.

Signora Cellini was sleeping, though not as peacefully as Jan would have wished. A damp crushed handkerchief lay in a beam of moonlight, eloquent of the tears Bianca's mother had shed. Jan drew a light chair up to the bed, and waited quietly till the restlessness passed and sleep deepened. Poor worried soul! She shouldn't be left alone yet. Am I justified, Jan wondered, in walking out on her because Marco has annoyed me? I'm a nurse and surely I've learned by now to put the patient's needs before my personal worries.

The moonbeam had moved halfway across the carpet before Jan was satisfied. Then she smoothed the sheets carefully, moved cautiously towards the paler patch which indicated the tall French windows which stood open on the terrace and garden. In the Villa Tramonti, house and garden blended together so cleverly that one could hardly tell where one ended and the other began.

It was almost as light as day outside. The moon still stood high, and the pale flush of pre-dawn was showing in the eastern sky. Jan drew in a deep breath of the morning air. She was tired at last, and thought she would be able to sleep.

Marco was standing there. The moonlight accentuated the darkness of his tan, silvered the light blue trousers and shirt. Jan stifled a startled exclamation. 'Marco! I thought you were a ghost!'

'No ghosts at the Villa Tramonti. Or if there are, they are not to be feared. Come and sit down. I want to talk to you.'

He turned and went towards the chairs without looking to see if she followed. She hesitated, longing now for her bed and sleep. She had had a tiring day, and been awake most of the night. This was no time for talking. Then she dismissed the attitude as petty, and followed her host. If he was now ready to talk, it would be stupid to miss the opportunity.

He had already drawn out a chair for her, and was waiting for her to sit down. As she approached he held out his hand and took hers lightly. It was no more than a courteous handing to her seat, but her heartbeat quickened with excitement and a certain amount of apprehension. What could they say to each other, here in the moonlight which warred with the dawn?

'You have been with my mother,' he began. 'Thank you, Jan. I looked in, twenty minutes ago, and saw you sitting by her bed.' He smiled at her. 'After all, you are a nurse before you are a woman. Which makes it easier for me to eat humble pie and beg you to stay with her. If you really loathe me, I can return to the Rome apartment, but my mother needs someone just now.'

'I was going to say the same to you.' Her cheeks burned. 'I behaved abominably, throwing those things at you, and I apologise. I don't loathe you, Marco, and I'll be glad to remain with your mother till the end of my holiday. But I can't stay longer. That is out of the question. As you say, I'm a nurse first, and duty means a lot to me. At this distance and in these surroundings, one unimportant nurse among so many may seem not to matter. But it does matter. Hospitals are chronically short-staffed. If I don't turn up on the right day, someone else's holiday, or off-duty times, will be affected. I'd be enjoying myself here while another girl works extra hard to make up for it.'

'I understand. You think I'm selfish, putting my needs first?'

'You are concerned for your mother—that's natural. You must consider getting some sort of nurse for her to take my place, at least until your sister comes home. Your private affairs are no business of mine, but—*is* she coming home, Marco? Is it true you don't know where she is? If you can talk to me about it—if I can help in any way, please do. You've tried to be father and mother both, haven't you?'

'As you see.' He shrugged lightly. 'Not very successfully. She was betrothed, and seemed happy about it. Raf is a charming young man, and his family welcomed her. It's a good match. So why should she suddenly take off into the blue—run away without letting us know where she is?'

'With another man?'

'That's what I fear. But who? She has met so few, and all of them known to me, of course.'

'Have you been to the police? Are you sure she's even safe?'

'The police, yes. I've searched myself, and Dino has scoured every inch of the island, all the rocks and caves. We've ruled out any possibility of an accident, though we never stop searching.'

'How long has she been missing?'

'Two days before you came. When I saw you, I thought I'd found her. You have the same way of walking, the same proud lift of the head, and almost the same colouring. I asked you here on an impulse, thinking if you were here we could cover up for a day or two, till she decided to come home.'

'So it was a masquerade?'

He nodded. 'Unplanned, and, I see now, foolish. It wasn't fair to you.'

'It was not. I was very angry when I found you'd been making use of me in that way. What I don't understand is why you needed to cover up. Surely some publicity about a missing girl would have helped? Newspapers, television—in our country we'd have used all that, to locate her.'

' My dear girl! Publicity is the last thing we want. Rafaello and his family would never accept that; to have her name bandied about, people staring at her photograph. I wouldn't do that to Bianca. There would be a scandal, her reputation would suffer. The engagement would be broken off.'

She could hardly believe he was serious. ' You mean —her fiancé doesn't know? You haven't asked him if he knows where she is?'

' We protect our young ladies. The permissive society has not yet penetrated into some of our more traditional families. Raf will expect a bride of unblemished reputation.'

There was a long silence. A bird cheeped as the light strengthened.

At last Jan asked quietly, ' Why did she run away, Marco?'

' We quarrelled.' His voice was weary. ' She didn't want to marry Raf.'

' And you insisted?'

' Yes. She had accepted him. She had nothing against him. And we do not break promises. I put the whole thing down to a girlish whim and told her to behave herself. This is not just a fisher-lad and a village girl. Both families have great responsibilities—wealth and big estates. Bianca has been educated for such responsibilities. She can't play childish games with such important matters. She understands all that, or I thought she did. She's no fool.'

' If she's no fool, she had her reasons. You didn't listen?'

' She didn't offer any reasons. She just said she wouldn't marry him, and nothing I could say made any

84

difference.'

'That sounds as if you did all the talking. Did you, just once, shut up and let Bianca talk? Do you know what I'm thinking, Marco? She's in love with another man. No, let me finish. You say she had nothing against Raf, and understood all that such a marriage entailed, so naturally she'd need to have the strongest of all possible reasons for wanting to break it off. And that could only be that she was deeply in love with someone else.'

He did not answer at once. The rim of the sun was showing above the horizon, and the angle of light revealed the hard masculine bone structure, the deep lines of anxiety.

'You're a woman,' he said at last. 'You should be able to read a woman's mind. Do you think she is with him now? That they are married?'

'From what you have told me of Bianca, I'd say not. I think this is an effort to make you understand that she must choose for herself; and that she is prepared to give up everything, if she must, to marry the man she loves. Perhaps an attempt to make you understand that even old families like yours cannot live for ever in the past. But I don't think she'd get married without your freely given consent, Marco.'

'So she is resorting to emotional blackmail?'

'Weren't you? Didn't you twist her arm to make her marry the man you'd chosen for her? Not physically, of course, but emotionally. Honour of the family, the responsibilities of great estates, and all that? Fair's fair in love and war. She is playing your game, Marco, and playing it well.'

'But if she'd told me—'

'Maybe she tried. Maybe she knew it wouldn't be any good trying. He's probably neither wealthy nor noble, but just a nice ordinary boy she loves. Find her, Marco. Get a message to her somehow, letting her know you will listen to what she has to say. Because she's going to win, whatever you say. You may as well accept that as a fact.'

He pushed back his chair, stood up abruptly. 'You've been up all night. Time I let you go and get some sleep. You've given me a lot to think about, and you may well be right. I don't know how women think, and perhaps I didn't handle the situation very well. It's been—difficult. You see how my mother is— not really of this world any more. I did my best, but it wasn't good enough, was it? You've changed your mind about leaving today?'

'If I'm forgiven for throwing things at my host, I'd like to stay.'

He held out his hand and after a brief hesitation she placed hers in it. His fingers closed over hers, and she was aware of the leap of her blood, the racing pulse, as she felt his warmth and strength. Then, without a word, almost without movement, he took her into his arms and there was nothing uncertain about the way he kissed her. Held closely in his arms, his lips hard on hers, feeling the warmth of his body and with the man-scent of him in her nostrils, it seemed as if her cup of joy was full.

Then the joy drained away, replaced by despair. The kiss had done nothing but deepen the feeling she had for him, the need of her body, the yearning of her heart. But there was no future in this love. How could he, with his rigid ideas of tradition, of the importance of wealth and estates in a marriage contract, ever think of marriage with a penniless working girl from another country, another culture?

And neither he nor she could accept anything less. She had perfect confidence that he would not cheapen her, although she must seem like beggarmaid to his king; nor would she cheapen herself.

The end of the holiday, the end of her time at Villa

Tramonti, could not come too soon. For her peace of mind, any hope of happiness she had in the future, it was imperative she should get away as soon as possible.

Yet every remaining hour was precious. They were all she would ever have of Marco's presence. The next few days had to last her the rest of her life.

CHAPTER V

Jan woke slowly, drowsily aware of Francesca standing by her bedside with a tray; of a delicious smell of coffee and hot rolls.

'It is almost lunchtime, *signorina*, but the Signore said to bring coffee but not to disturb you if you were asleep.'

Recollection flooded back. Jan sat up. 'The Signora? How is she? She was not well last night, Francesca, which is why I did not get to bed till nearly morning. The Signore should have sent you to wake me hours ago.'

'The Signora is well. She had breakfast in bed, and is now in the garden. She—' the girl hesitated, then burst out with what she wanted to say. 'My mistress is sick, *signorina*. She remembers nothing one tells her. And she is sad because Signorina Bianca is not here.'

'Where is Signorina Bianca?' Jan put the question sharply, with a vague idea that the young girl might know, or suspect, where another young girl had sought refuge.

The girl shrugged expressively. Jan was beginning to learn something of the infinite variations of Italian shrug, and interpreted this one as meaning *How should I know?* But, she noted, Francesca did not come out with the stock answer that Bianca was visiting her aunt in Florence.

Jan narrowed her eyes, watching the girl. Maybe she knows something. Maybe everyone but Marco knows. The servants, especially the women, must have known of the battle of wills going on between Bianca and her brother.

Jan poured her coffee. 'Is the Signorina Bianca beautiful? I'd like to see a photograph of her. There must be one somewhere.'

' *Si, si.* Have you not seen it? A big coloured picture, where she was bridesmaid at the wedding last summer? There is one in the Signore's room. I will fetch it to show you.'

' No, Francesca, wait! Do not disturb the Signore. Perhaps Signora Cellini has one in her room.'

The girl shook her head. ' Signore Cellini took them away when his sister went. If there are no photographs, she does not remember to ask for her daughter all the time, only sometimes. The Signore has gone to Naples with Dino. I can fetch the picture. He will not be back all day.'

The wedding picture showed the bride and four bridesmaids. The bridesmaids wore long-sleeved, high-waisted dresses in deep cream silk with brown velvet sashes, and carried sprays of cream roses. Jan drew a deep breath.

' She's beautiful, Francesca. One day she'll be a bride herself.'

' *Si signorina.*' Expressionless. Not the voice of a girl talking weddings.

When the girl had disappeared with the photograph, Jan buttered her rolls absently, thinking. A young married friend? The other bridesmaids could be dismissed. Obviously daughters living at home and, however sympathetic to romance, not able to shelter a runaway. But the bride? There was a possibility.

How am I so sure that Bianca has not eloped, and is not now married to her sweetheart? Is it because I am living in her rooms, wearing her clothes, am supposed to look something like her, that I imagine I can feel as she does? She loves her mother and brother, she doesn't want to hurt them permanently, or bring disgrace on the family. Of that I'm sure. So this is a protest only, a cry for help.

Pushing the tray aside, Jan pressed her fingers to her

temples. Think, think! Somewhere there must be a clue to the girl's mind, if only I could read it. No one disappears entirely without trace. Especially—

She sat up straight, startled by a thought. Especially if she really wants her protest to be noticed. What's the good of a demonstration if no one sees it? If only Marco had told me the whole story at the beginning, we might have found the solution by now.

She was still puzzling over the problem as she dived into the pool and swam lazily. When she floated, she reflected that the all-over golden tan she had acquired would be the envy of her friends, and that the tan would fade long before the memories of last night; of all the hours she had spent in Marco Cellini's company.

Signora Cellini was in her favourite spot on the terrace overlooking the sea. She had her needlework in her lap, but her hands were folded over the delicate silks, and she stared out to sea like a blind woman. Jan stood unnoticed, watching the older woman, and the change in her overnight caught at her heart. The Signora seemed to have shrunk since yesterday. The frail bones showed clearly through the thin black dress; shoulderblades and vertebrae.

Enough is enough, Jan thought. She's had all she can take. Bianca must come home. Marco must forget all his scruples about publicity. If he doesn't find his sister soon, his mother will slip through his fingers.

She went forward and knelt beside the old lady, who lifted heavy lids to look at her. The disappointment in the sharp old eyes brought a lump to Jan's throat.

'You've finished the passion flower,' she said gently, touching the embroidery, noting the skin of the long narrow fingers was thin as paper. 'Is it for Bianca? It's a screen, isn't it?'

She had a theory which she half feared to test. But now, if ever, was the time. The matter of Bianca's return was urgent.

The fine brows drew together, as if an effort to remember was being made. ' A screen, for a *salone*. My daughter is to have a splendid establishment, you know. She is to be a countess, and live in a *palazzo*. She must take many beautiful things with her.'

' Of course, *signora*.' Jan moistened dry lips. ' Where is she now, *signora*?'

Again that knitting of the brows, ' I don't remember.'

' But she did tell you where she was going?'

' Oh yes, of course. Bianca tells me everything. I am her mother.'

Jan's heart turned over. As she thought! The Signora knew but had forgotten. Somewhere in that lost mind lay the information so sorely needed. Questioning would not help. The Signora would only become more confused if pressed. Jan pulled a cushion towards her, tucked her legs under, and spoke casually of this and that, always leading the talk back to travel, to Bianca's friends, to the wedding picture which the Signora remembered well, and talked about in an animated way. Till suddenly she fell silent and began that unseeing stare at the blue horizon again.

The gate to the cliff path was unlocked. Jan's gaze came back to it again and again. Had Bianca gone that way? But it led nowhere, except to a beach and though Mahco had admitted it was possible to swim round the headland, it seemed an unlikely journey for a girl bent on leaving home and presumably wanting clothes with her.

How did Bianca get off the island?

Jan sat up straight, ignoring her hostess, who had started on a long tale about the Cellinis of long ago. Why hadn't I asked Marco that? No doubt he took it for granted, as I did, that Bianca had slipped on board the once-a-week boat which brought supplies, mail, and a few visitors to Barini. He would have questioned the local boatmen. A few smart white yachts put in, from time to time, but the harbour was too small for anything ambitious.

One should never accept the obvious. Bianca might have gone some other way. Someone might have fetched her, perhaps from the beach below. It would be easier to make a secret getaway from one's own garden than to walk on to the supply boat carrying a suitcase. Fifty people could have seen her, noticed that Signorina Cellini had luggage, speculated on her destination. In a peasant community it was likely that no member of the Cellini family left the villa for any purpose, without being noticed and discussed.

The beach, then? The only place a Cellini could leave unnoticed. Jan promised herself that as soon as the villa settled to the afternoon siesta, she would go down and look around, even if it meant braving that sheer ladder alone.

Before lunch, when she went to tidy her hair and add a skirt to the brief swimsuit in which she had spent the morning, Jan riffled through the long fitted wardrobe, wondering not for the first time what Bianca had taken with her. If there were gaps, they were not evident.

She looked again at the pretty beauty box full of make-up. Bianca liked experimenting, that was obvious. Shoes and sandals? Dozens of them. Whatever the girl had seen fit to take, it had not made much impact on her ample stock of lovely clothes. She had travelled light. Why? She did not seem like the simple-life type.

Somewhere in these two rooms lay the clue to their owner's whereabouts; a clue, that is, to her thinking and planning. Marco would not know. He was too much of a man to know much about a woman's clothes.

Francesca? It was too near lunchtime now to ring

for the girl, but at the next opportunity Jan resolved to question her. Meantime, the beach.

When all the villa was sunk in the silence of the afternoon siesta, Jan crept down the path to the hidden beach. Tight-lipped, she tackled the ladder. Once on the rungs, her face turned towards the rocks, it was not too bad. She fought the temptation to look down, and so was surprised when her groping foot touched sand instead of iron. She blew out a sigh of relief.

The sand was warm and soft. The sea turquoise in the shallows, emerald over the rocks and seaweed farther out; and then that intense, brilliant blue that only the Bay of Naples can be. But it was empty. The tiny bay, cupped between tiny headlands, was silent except for the sibilant whisper of the water among the rocks.

Could a boat land? She paddled along the white ruffles of foam, head down, thinking hard. Thinking herself into another girl's mind. Then inevitably, her thoughts came round to Marco Cellini and her own imminent departure for home.

It was her own choice to go. She had only to say the word, and this life in the sun was hers. Marco could be generous about salary. The duties would not be onerous. And she would be within sight and sound of the man she loved, for as long as she chose to stay.

So why go back to an English winter, the long hours in the wards, the examinations still to come?

Luxury, ease, sunshine, and a good salary were hers for the taking. So why not say yes? Why not take a chance that one day, sooner or later, Marco Cellini might fall in love with her? Stranger things had happened. The man was not indifferent to her—his kisses proved that.

True, they had quarrelled. But they had also made up their quarrels, and grown a little in understanding by doing so. They had been good companions on occasion; talking, exchanging ideas, arguing, laughing. Such beginnings could blossom into love.

Whereas if she took the long tiresome train and ship journey home, there would be no chance at all for her. Why be such a fool, Jan Lynton?

Ankle-deep in creaming foam, she had almost reached the rocks at one side of the bay. Shading her eyes, she scanned them carefully for a cranny where a boat might be concealed. Nothing. The rock went sheer into the water, the cracks in it big enough to grow a clump of valerian or broom, no more.

Turning, she kicked up a small shell and stopped to pick it up. The small, exquisitely sculpted thing lay on her palm, outside creamy white, the lining rosy and lustrous as a pink pearl. As she examined it with delight, a pair of strong male arms clasped her tightly; a man's voice, certainly not Marco's, poured out a flood of rapid Italian. She could feel his breath in her hair.

She screamed at the top of her voice, kicked backwards viciously with her heel, and felt it jar on what she hoped was her attacker's shin.

Instantly she was released. A large brown hand steadied her when she staggered and almost fell.

' *Santo cielo! Cosa fa?* You are not Bianca!'

' I am not Bianca,' she agreed crossly. ' And you are trespassing. This is a private beach. How did you get here and what are you doing?'

She spoke to the intruder in the tones Sister Macfarlane used to a tiresome patient, unconsciously adopting Sister's intimidating stance, shoulders back, chin high, eyes blazing. That she was clad in a pink bikini instead of the crisp uniform of St Cleo's made little difference. The young man was abashed.

' I'm sorry,' he said meekly. ' It was a mistake.'

He was about twenty-five, she reckoned. Dark, slender, black hair curling neatly into his neck and

94

making him look like a Greek statue. Blue eyes in an olive-skinned face. Eyes and mouth which were almost laughing in spite of the penitent attitude and humble apology.

Jan pointed her finger at him, exclaiming: 'You thought I was Bianca! So you must be Bianca's boy-friend? I mean—' she frowned, searching for the right words, 'you love Bianca?'

The boy straightened and bowed, as if in some elegant drawing-room. 'I have that honour, *signorina*.'

'At last! Well, where is she?'

'I don't understand. Is the Signorina Bianca not at home?'

'You know quite well she isn't. She has been missing for over a week. Her brother is almost out of his mind with worry, but that's not so important as her mother. Will you please stop playing games and bring her home? Don't pretend. This is serious. Her mother *needs* her—she is ill.'

The boy said nothing. He stared at Jan, and if a suntanned olive skin can whiten, that was what happened. The blood drained from his face and for a moment Jan thought he would drop into the water in a dead faint. He closed his eyes tightly, shook his head like a dog emerging from a bath.

'Missing? Bianca is missing? But where is she? Is no one searching for her? Has she had an accident? *Santo cielo!* She might be drowned.'

'She might,' Jan agreed gravely. 'But we don't think so. I thought she might be with you.'

The boy was shocked. 'But never! That would not be discreet, and Bianca is a young lady well brought up. I would never ask her to do such a thing—never.'

'But you've been meeting her secretly, here on this beach? Is that discreet?'

He spread eloquent hands. '*Signorina*, we love each

95

other!'

'And I suppose you swam round the headland, in the best traditions of Hero and Leander? Very romantic—but becoming serious if Bianca doesn't come back soon. You'd better tell me all you know. Shall we sit down in the shade and talk? My name is Jan Lynton and I'm English, as you will have guessed from my shaky Italian.'

'You speak very good Italian—for an English-woman. I am Paolo Ricardo, employed in the Cellini concern.' His smile flashed. 'One of their bright young men, supposed to have a big future. But nevertheless, one of the hired hands, and so not acceptable as a match for the daughter of the Cellini house.'

'Why not? Our princesses are allowed to marry commoners these days, if it's a love match. What is good enough for the British royal family should be good enough for Marco Cellini.'

'Perhaps you will tell him so, *signorina?*'

'I certainly will, given a chance. Now let's get out of this water and conduct a proper conversation. There's a useful rock over there, and if you'd be kind enough to fetch my wrap from the foot of the ladder, there are cigarettes in the pocket.'

'Bianca and I met at one of the firm's social functions,' Paolo began, when they were comfortably settled in the shade of the rock. 'We fell in love that evening. We both knew it was foolish, wrong. She was already affianced. But love, *signorina*, love is like the wind. Who can tell when it will blow, and in what direction; who can stop it?'

'It was for you to be wise and strong, for her sake, Paolo. You should never have met again.'

'Easy to say, when one is not in love. But when one is? We met in the Farnese Gardens in Rome—just once. And then again, to say goodbye. And then—'

'Then you started swimming?' Jan's sympathy was wholly with the lovers, caught between the overwhelming power of young love and the rigid traditions of a proud family, a binding engagement. Romeo and Juliet, struggling in a cruel net.

'I keep a boat, in Ischia harbour. It is anchored just around the rocks there. We have been waiting till Bianca could extricate herself from the engagement to Rafaello. She hoped her brother would listen to her, but he was so angry when she even mentioned the matter.' He turned to look into Jan's face. 'Bianca is not very brave, *signorina*. She is afraid of her brother.'

'Why? He seems a reasonable man, and young. Surely if she told him she was in love with someone else, he would at least try to understand.'

'Ah, but he has never been in love himself, she says. One day he may learn about the pain of loving, and be more sympathetic. As a matter of fact, Bianca has not mentioned me.'

'I thought not. Why?'

He shrugged. 'I am an employee, completely in the Signore's power.'

'You mean he'd sack you? But that's not fair. And even if he did, would that matter? You say you're one of the firm's bright boys? I suppose that means management trainee or something? If you're good enough for the Cellini undertaking, you're good enough for anyone else. There must be big opportunities for brains in the Common Market.'

'That's what I tell Bianca. But she is afraid of what Marco Cellini might do, to ruin my career. We Italians are not tolerant people; we feel intensely, and hit our enemies hard. Cellini has much power. So she is afraid for me.'

He stubbed out his cigarette in the sand and turned towards Jan. '*Signorina*, I have told you too much. You will tell the Signore everything? Whatever he does to me will not matter, if Bianca is found. You understand that?'

'Yes, I do, Paolo. I want to keep your secret, but I am in a dilemma. I am Marco Cellini's guest, he has been kind to me. To keep your secret means betraying his hospitality. You do see that?'

'Yes. But if it must be so, it must be. I myself am willing to face him any time, and ask him for his sister's hand in marriage. But he will simply tell me that she is not free and I have no right to ask. What he does to me after that is unimportant. As you say, I can find other employment, perhaps in another country. Bianca wishes us to go gently, to take no risks. She believes she can win him round in the end.'

Jan let the fine soft sand trickle through her fingers. She did not answer at once.

'Paolo,' she said at last, 'I believe Bianca is right. From what I know of Marco, he will not be rushed into an important decision like this. I will give you a little longer, but if Bianca is not back in two days, I must tell. Now, let us put our heads together and think. Where is she?'

'I swear I do not know.'

'Do you think she ran away to try and bring Marco round; to make him understand she really meant it when she said she wouldn't marry Raf?'

'She is capable of that. If they had a quarrel—if she lost patience—she is a passionate and self-willed girl in some ways. Gentle and loving, too. It has been hard for her.'

'They did quarrel—Marco told me. The next day she was gone. Think, Paolo. Think hard. Where did she go? What friends has she?'

'Few of her own age. Giulia and Pietro in Frascati would sympathise and hide her. She'd be safe with them. Otherwise—' he shrugged, 'I don't know. Rome is full of hippies, and wandering young people of all countries, but Bianca wouldn't go to them. She is too—fastidious.'

'You don't think she's in any danger?'

'Not of her own making. She is shrewd, mostly. She may have bolted on impulse, but she'd choose a good bolthole.'

'How do you think she got off the island?'

'That has been puzzling me. She's so well known here.' He stood up, stretched his arms above his head as if he could not contain his energy. 'We are wasting time, Signorina Jan. I must go at once, and start searching for her. I shall try Giulia and Pietro today. Be sure I shall not sleep for an hour until she is found.'

'Who were the bride and groom of last year's wedding, where she was bridesmaid?'

He grinned ruefully. 'Too grand for me! But it's a good idea. Can you suggest that to the Signore?'

'I intended to. He is away from the island today, but as soon as he comes home, I shall. In two days, Paolo, I shall tell him everything. You understand?' He nodded and she went on, 'I am wrong not to tell him today. I owe him that much loyalty, and I know little about you. So I shall not give you one hour beyond the time. Two days.'

He bowed formally. '*Signorina*, in two days I shall present myself at the Villa Tramonti and speak to Marco Cellini myself, whether Bianca is found or not. I am not afraid of him myself—only for Bianca. She has begged me not to speak to him, but I am a man and now I must do what is right, whatever she says. If a woman rules a man too long, she begins to despise him.'

'Well done, Paolo! Now I begin to see why Bianca ran away. You sound like a man worth waiting for. Good luck then.'

He kissed her hand lightly, then waded thigh-deep into the water, then came back. 'Have you considered that Bianca may not have left the island after all? She may be here somewhere.'

'I thought of it. But who would dare hide her?'

'The Cellinis don't own everything. And everybody doesn't love them, *signorina*. It would be worth while looking right under Marco's nose.'

Then he plunged into the sea and swam away, with a strong, slow stroke. In the clear water he was visible almost to the headland. She waited till, after what seemed a painfully long time she heard the chug of an engine, and knew he was safely on his way to Ischia.

So half Bianca's secret, the important half, had been revealed. The other half would follow, Jan was certain. Bianca would be found, or come home. Or Paolo would bring her.

What would Marco's reactions be, when he knew the whole truth? How could a man who had never been in love understand the hurt and the glory of it? The need to be together. The awfulness of the never-never!

It was a thousand pities for Bianca that Paolo had come into her life. If she hadn't gone to the party that fatal night, she'd be a happy girl now, choosing her trousseau and looking forward to marriage with the eligible Rafaello, to becoming a countess, to queening it over a splendid *palazzo*.

Too bad that an ordinary boy, a nice boy with a cheerful grin, turned up that night, and upset the whole pattern of her life. What magic was love, that it could do such a thing? What made the fatal difference between Raf and Paolo? And why only for Bianca?

She hauled herself over the last lap of the climb and sat on the terrace to recover her breath. Why Bianca with Paolo and nobody else? Why me—with Marco, the unattainable? Is it because they are unattainable that we fall in love with them?

Forbidden fruit. Out of reach. Was that part of

the magic, then? Jan's own experience among the students and nurses had proved over and over again that easy-come too often meant easy-go. If she and Michael had had to fight for each other, wait, hope, and fret, maybe that first bright flash of love might have kindled a steadier glow.

Dino was back. Seeing him in the garden, Jan asked if the Signore had returned with him. The boy set down the big watering-can carefully, to pull out a weed. 'Assuredly, *signorina*. He is a good son, like all Italians, and he will not leave his *mamma* too long alone at this time.' He began his evening task of watering again.

'While his sister is away? Dino, if you should happen to see the Signorina Bianca, tell her her mother is like a flower without water. She has been long enough without water. You understand?'

Dino looked at her, blandly innocent. 'How should I see her? I have searched the island for her, in the boat and on land. Unless I go with the Signore, I never leave Barini except at *festa* time, when we all go to Capri or Sorrento. How can I tell the young mistress anything?'

'I don't know, Dino. But keep the message in mind, you and the other servants. Just in case you happen to see her.'

He grinned happily and nodded, then moved along the flowerbeds with his can and weeding fork. I'm wasting my time, Jan thought, but *somebody* knows. Somebody on the island. Ten to one the message will reach her.

To Jan's dismay, Signora Cellini decided to retire early and have dinner in bed on a tray. That meant a *diner à deux* with Marco. And after the events of last night, or rather early in the morning, she would have preferred the usual arrangements of mother and son discussing the events of the day, and herself acting the silent and tactful companion, speaking when spoken to but not pushing herself forward.

'I think,' she said when sitting at table could no longer be postponed, 'I will sit with your mother. Perhaps Francesca will bring me something on a tray, too.'

He drew out a chair. 'You will sit and eat your dinner like a civilised person. Francesca can stay with Mamma for a while. Is she worse?'

'No. But under strain. Even in a week, Marco, she looks older, more tired and thinner. It would be wise, perhaps, to have her doctor over.'

The first course was asparagus, smothered in butter and topped with a poached egg. Jan was too nervous to taste anything, though asparagus was a rare treat and unknown in the Nurses' Hostel.

'I'll send for him tomorrow.'

They ate in silence for a while. Not a companionable silence, such as they had experienced on occasion. This was a stiff, uncomfortable meal. She wondered what was in his mind. Was he remembering the kisses he had pressed upon her, on this very terrace, at dawn? Or was his mind far away in Rome, occupied with the business problems of the day just ended?

'You are quiet,' he said at last. 'But then you must be tired. You sat up late with my mother last night. Believe me, I am grateful.'

'I'm accustomed to night duty. Marco, I—'

Her throat dried up and she could not speak. He watched her, enquiringly.

'Well? You were going to say something?'

'Only that it seems imperative that your sister comes home. I think your mother is fretting more than appears on the surface. There's a deterioration in her condition.'

'Have you any ideas? I'm doing all I can.' His

tone was icy.

'You know her friends. I don't. But it seemed to me she might go to a young person, who would understand how she felt, and also have the facilities for sheltering her. I mean, a young married friend with a home of her own. Have you considered that?'

His eyes narrowed. 'It's an idea, and I confess it had not occurred to me. The difficulty is that one cannot telephone all one's acquaintances and ask if they have a missing girl in the house.'

'Why not?'

'Because they will instantly telephone all their friends and relations and announce that Bianca Cellini has run away. In twenty-four hours the news would be all over Rome and beyond. A dozen women would have spoken to Rafaello's mother and sisters, and Raf would be here demanding to know what had happened. And, probably, breaking off the engagement.'

'He doesn't love her,' Jan said with a rush. 'Oh, Marco, we've been talking about Bianca's feelings all this time—whether she was in love with another man, why she didn't want Raf, what made her run away. Have you never once thought of it the other way round? I confess I hadn't. If this man truly loved Bianca, he wouldn't give a damn for publicity, or whether she'd popped off to visit a friend without telling Mum, or *what*. In your heart, you know it. That's why you're afraid of letting this splendid match slip through your fingers. You know he doesn't love her. He's marrying her for your money!'

There was a tiny silver salt-cellar on the table, fashioned in the shape of a swan. Marco pushed it backwards and forwards, concentrating on it in tight-lipped silence. When he finally looked at her, his eyes were hooded, not a flicker of expression in them.

'That would make a difference? All the women of my family have always declared that love comes after a marriage; yes, even my mother's, though her marriage was an idyll to the very end. Can they all be wrong?'

'They could be lucky. If it worked for all of them, they *were* lucky. But haven't you overlooked an important factor in this theory of yours? Didn't they go into marriage with a man who loved them, who understood love and had the power to rouse it in them? Did your father love your mother? Were you told that?'

His dark eyes flickered. 'He had adored her for two years. He first saw her as a schoolgirl and made up his mind to marry her as soon as she was old enough.'

'There you are, then! He wanted to win her love. He did his courting after they were married, and was brilliantly successful. But Raf—does he want Bianca as badly as your father wanted the girl he loved? Will he woo her, gently and tenderly? Will she come first in his heart? It matters, Marco. It matters most terribly to a woman.' She spoke urgently and with stirred emotions.

He gave her a dry, wry smile. 'This is a change of tune on your part. Are you now prepared to say that a marriage could succeed if there was love on one side only? You have been so passionately against our way of arranging marriages up to now.'

'If there is a courtship, from one who truly loves— yes, it could succeed after marriage as it often succeeds before. Fashions change, but women don't change their basic needs. And one of those basic needs is for tenderness, for a touch of splendour, a little romance. A man who will give her that will win her heart for ever. She likes her love like champagne in a Venetian goblet, to show that she is valued. Once she's sure of that one fact, she'll be happy enough to share cocoa in a cracked kitchen cup.' She added thoughtfully, 'One could start off with the cocoa and the cracked cup, so long as there was enough loving to make believe it was champagne and crystal.'

'And you think—without having seen him—that Raf is incapable of this?'

'He may provide the Venetian glass, the diamonds, and the golden shoes, in a material way. I'm sure he would. Orchids, too. But I'm not talking about that. I'm talking about the heart, Marco. If you knew he wanted Bianca more than anything in the whole wide world—more than money, or status, or power, or a beautiful woman to grace his *palazzo*—you'd have sent for him the moment she disappeared. But you didn't. It is you who have condemned him, not I.'

The guilt she felt at deceiving Marco about the appearance of Paolo had evaporated. She was wholly on the side of the young lovers, now she had understood about the unknown Rafaello. She was merely angry with him, and with Marco for being so blind.

'Of course,' she went on more quietly, 'you yourself have never been in love, so you can't possibly know.'

His mouth twisted into a half-smile, but his eyes were sad. 'Why do you say that, with such confidence? With such arrogance, and such inaccuracy. I assure you I know what it means to love, and to have the woman I love completely out of reach.'

Colour suffused her face and throat. Without thinking, she touched his hand as it lay on the table beside the silver salt-cellar. 'You are right to call me arrogant, Marco. I'm deeply sorry, believe me. I had no business to say such a stupid thing, even though I believed it true. Can you forgive me?'

'Easily,' he said briskly, sitting up straight and casting a glance over the table like an efficient host. 'Now let us forget the whole thing. This is your holiday and you should not burden yourself with my troubles. You have given me an idea and tomorrow I shall carry it out. Bianca's friend Gina is a young married woman and would have sympathy with her in this escapade. We shall go and call on her tomorrow. Luckily she lives on Capri, so if you will accompany me, I will show you the island as I promised. It will be a pleasant expedition for you.'

She drew back, disappointed by his sudden change of tone. A moment before, she had been in his confidence and able to speak to him freely of what was in her mind. Now, the door was closed firmly in her face. She was on the outside, a visitor to be entertained.

'There is no need to take me,' she said stiffly. 'I am enjoying my holiday here, at the villa.'

'There is every need,' he replied coolly. 'You will provide the excuse for my calling on Gina. I shall ask her to show our guest her beautiful home and her special view of the Bay. You didn't think I'd just ring her bell and ask for Bianca, did you?'

He needed help, and she knew now that he would never ask it. Rather, he would simply tell her what he wanted and expect her to conform. She laughed lightly to conceal her disappointment. 'Stupidly, I did think just that. How have you managed all this time, Marco? In your search, I mean. Don't tell me if you don't want to.'

'I've had private detectives—not those television types in old raincoats, but the best. The men who can move in exclusive circles without being noticed, expensive, highly-trained, discreet. Also I've visited aunts and cousins, second cousins and distant in-laws. For family, one doesn't need an excuse, only a box of Zia Flavia's favourite chocolates and some cigars for one's uncle. Believe me, I have been a dutiful relative lately, eaten more family meals, sampled more wine from family vineyards, listened to more family history, than I have done in the last twenty years. But not a sign of Bianca anywhere. Also, I hope and trust, not a suspicion of the true state of affairs.'

'Poor Marco,' she murmured softly. 'You have suffered a great deal, and now I have hurt you.'

He gave her hand a quick, friendly squeeze. 'And I have forgiven you, so let us forget it and get on with this excellent rib of beef.'

The discussion was over. From then on, Marco talked of many things, none of them personal. The history of ancient Rome, the luxury and degeneracy of the latter days of the empire and the emperors; Pompeii, the city which died and was preserved for posterity in one terrible day of fear and fire.

'There is so much you haven't seen yet, Jan. Yet you are determined to leave it all, at the end of the week?'

'The week is racing away. The end is almost here. We ought to talk over my travel arrangements soon. May I show you the documents tomorrow? A bus is supposed to pick me up at the Rome hotel and—'

'Tomorrow we go to Capri. This time we are really going. I've promised too often already, and you cannot leave the Bay of Naples without seeing all our jewels.'

Barini is enough for me, she thought, if you are here. But she put the thought firmly from her.

CHAPTER VI

In the early morning sunlight, the harbour at Barini looked quaint and charming, and Jan's heart ached at the sight of it. It didn't look 'foreign' at all. In some strange way, and in such a short time, Barini had become home, from which she was shortly to be exiled.

Dino had the boat ready, and Marco handed her in with a cheerful smile. He was wearing white shorts today, with brown leather sandals and a pink shirt. Jan had chosen the prettiest of her own dresses, a halter-neck lime green cotton, and tied a matching scarf round her hair. Marco approved when she handed him a white blazer, remarking that there was always a cool breeze on the water. The blazer Jan had been obliged to borrow from Bianca's wardrobe, but she planned not to take it ashore at Capri.

A puzzling thing had happened before breakfast. The cornflower blue trouser suit she had worn on her first day seemed to be missing from the wardrobe. Francesca had disclaimed knowledge of it.

'But you must remember, Francesca. It was here, next to the white blazer. I wore it myself. Did you take it away to be washed, perhaps?'

The girl shook her head obstinately. Had she genuinely forgotten, or was that stubborn look her defence against being accused of making away with something, perhaps? Or did she know where the suit had vanished, and was determined not to tell?

'I'm not cross about it, Francesca,' Jan had said gently. 'You're not in trouble. These clothes are not mine. I'd like to know if it is safe, that's all. Maybe you put it in another room?'

The girl burst into tears and said she'd always been honest, and her mother before her; that if she lost her job at the villa her family would starve. It took Jan ten precious minutes to stem the flood of tears and denials, and comfort Francesca with a handful of lire.

All the same, that sunny shade of blue *had* hung next to the blazer, and now was not there.

Marco seemed to have put all his troubles aside and to be determined to make the day a happy one. As the boat left the harbour, he began to sing and presently Dino's voice joined his. Both men sang well, a lilting Neapolitan song with a refrain.

As he sang, Marco's eyes met Jan's, and they were laughing. This, she thought with quick delight, is the real Marco. Marco happy, unworried, not laden with the cares of everyday life. If only life could be like this, skimming over the smooth sea and singing!

I am happy *now*, she reminded herself. This is happening to me, at this minute. Hold it, keep it in the memory. The laughing brown faces, the sparkle of sun on the water, and Marco happy as a boy.

> *Music when soft voices die,*
> *Vibrates in the memory . . .*

But this music will have to do a great deal of vibrating, because memory is all I'm going to have of it. She blinked away the traitor tears which came without warning.

'Sing again, Marco,' she begged when the song was over. 'Just one more.'

He laughed and shouted to Dino. But Dino shook his head and said the Signore must sing alone now, for the lady. So Marco sang a love song which started happily and ended on a sad note.

'We can't be sad on a day like this,' he shouted to Dino. 'Come on, you lazy creature, cheer the lady up!'

They sang another duet, a brisk and lively air which had Jan tapping her feet. Then Marco left the boat to the boy and came to sit beside Jan.

'Enjoying yourself? I want you to have a good day. I've bothered you with my troubles too much, and I'm afraid you've found me short-tempered sometimes. If so, I apologise. It isn't your fault my mother is sick, and my sister has chosen to make this odd demonstration. So if you can forgive me—'

'Forgive you? Oh, Marco, you've been so thoughtful in so many ways. And I've been a bit tiresome at times, I admit. Let's forgive each other, shall we?'

He looked at her closely, thoughtfully. 'So you don't find me altogether a bear?'

Impulsively, she laid a hand on his. 'I find you a good friend and a good singer. This is really fun, and who knows, we may end the day by finding Bianca, too. I feel just a little guilty about your mother, though. Will she be all right alone?'

'Dino is taking the boat on to Sorrento, to collect two nuns whom she knows. I telephoned the Mother Superior this morning. The sisters will enjoy the outing, and Mama will be happy playing hostess. They will keep her entertained without talking too much, and make sure she rests. Satisfied?'

'Perfectly.'

There was also the question of what was to be done about his mother after Bianca married, but Jan did not ask it. It was not her affair, and Marco was capable of solving the problem in his own way when the time came. Today was to be a day when he relaxed and forgot, for a few hours, all his troubles. He had earned a holiday.

They talked little for the rest of the journey, but their silence was a friendly, companionable one, easy as an old shoe. When they put into the harbour at Capri, he gave Dino orders to fetch them at six, then hurried Jan along the quayside, dodging at top speed through the crowd of tourists.

'Where are we going?' she demanded, breathless.

110

'To the Blue Grotto, of course. What are those nurses going to say, if you admit to being on Capri and not seeing our grotto? Mind you, it's much exaggerated in my opinion, but it is definitely a grotto, and undeniably blue. We have to catch the sun at precisely the right angle, which is why—' He shouted and waved, whereupon a boat just taking off waited a moment for him to swing Jan aboard.

Soon they were chugging along, close in to the steep cliffs of the island, in a flotilla of motorboats carrying excited holidaymakers. 'We shall have to queue,' Marco said gloomily.

Jan did not care. The expedition might last all day, as far as she was concerned. She was with Marco, who seemed happy to be with her, and the day was wonderful, a day of silver and golden lights, of singing and gaiety and pure happiness.

Marco was right. At the entrance to the grotto, the boats had to wait for the smaller boats, as light and unstable as scallop shells, which collected passengers four by four, and disappeared under the low arch of the grotto. But at last their turn came.

'Into the bow,' Marco ordered. 'And lie down.' He followed her deftly, pulled her down low in the rocking boat, and laid his arm across her. 'Don't peek up till I tell you, or you may get a nasty bump on that attractive head of yours.'

The boatman pulled his craft along by a dripping iron chain overhead, and then, suddenly, they were in complete darkness. 'Wait, now,' Marco breathed in her ear. His breath moved her hair. To be so close to him, to be held so tightly, crouched low in this cockleshell, made her heart thump so hard that she feared he might hear it.

Then someone started singing, and the sound echoed round the cavern. 'I can't see a thing,' Jan whispered.

She felt rather than heard him chuckle. 'Now

look!'

They had turned to face the exit, and now at last she saw the breathtaking cerulean blue as the sun struck into the cave and lit the seemingly bottomless water, which danced with the movement of the boat.

'Oh, it's lovely, lovely!' she breathed.

He kissed her ear. 'So are you! Today suits you. You're wearing it like a new dress.' He chuckled again, and she knew the kiss meant nothing, only the irresistible temptation to kiss any fairly attractive girl when one's arm was round her, one's lips an inch from her ear. One did not attach importance to the odd kiss now and again, a light and delicate touch at a moment of special loveliness.

All too soon, the tiny boat emerged into full sunlight and made its way back to the parent craft. 'How on earth do they remember which one?' Jan wondered. 'There must be a hundred people here.'

And at least half the girls, she decided, had been kissed there in the convenient darkness of the grotto. It is probably a tradition, and unlucky the girl who doesn't find an arm round her, and a kiss for good measure. Well, I don't care. It is one more thing to remember. One more treasure in my jewel box.

One thing making it harder to forget Marco, she reminded herself sternly. One more thorn to pierce your heart, you fool!

Back at the harbour, Marco took a taxi up to the old town of Capri, and found a table at the restaurant in the tiny piazza. 'A pistachio ice, if I remember correctly? A large one, as it isn't nearly time for lunch.'

They lazed half an hour away, as Marco pointed out the curious arches of the church roof, the crowds constantly moving up and down the curved steps, the little shops.

'Decide what you would like for a souvenir,' he ordered. 'I intend to buy you a thank-you present for all you've done for Mamma.'

She smiled at him. 'This is my present, Marco—this day. The boat, and just sitting here, and this enormous ice, and—' she sighed contentedly. 'Everything. This is what we think of, back in England when we say Italy. Colour, warmth, flowers, fine old churches, and people. Like that old priest with the white beard, and the woman in black with the basket of bread.'

'You've been happy with me?'

'You know I have.'

He leaned towards her. 'Then why not stay, Jan *cara*? You know I want you to.'

She turned her face away, lest he should see naked longing in her eyes. 'You know I can't.'

That wasn't true. She could stay by saying the word. But she would be throwing away the last three years of hard work, and any hope of a future in nursing, such as she had planned. Throwing away, perhaps, the hope of marriage one day far ahead. For it was certain Marco Cellini would never consider the little nurse who cared for his mother as a possible bride. He would expect a fine dowry, an old, respected Italian family, possessions to match his own. Whoever he chose would be fortunate, for he would make that girl love him; exert all his charm, all the arts by which man woos woman, to make his wife his sweetheart and lover.

Yesterday he had said the woman he loved was out of reach. What did he mean by that? Maybe she was married already. Or dead, perhaps. But that would not stand in the way of his marriage when the time was ripe. He would need sons and daughters one day. The Italians, she had observed, adored children; and Marco, who looked nothing like a family man at this moment, would expect to surround himself with beautiful children in due course.

So she turned her head and said *I can't*, and died a

little as she spoke.

Presently he said it was time to move. 'Before lunch is a good time for our call. Leave the talking to me, but keep your eyes and ears open. If Bianca is there, we may be sure we shall see some trace of her. She's an untidy girl.'

'But she took so little. Why? That's what puzzles me. There's something at the back of my mind all the time, but I can never quite capture it. Some sort of clue.'

He was searching for a taxi. 'Something you saw?'

'No. At least, I don't think so. Something I heard. Did you ask me to do something which I haven't yet done?'

He halted by a railing. Far below lay the busy little harbour, the crowds milling slowly round and round, the orange-and-lemon stalls where vendors shouted their wares. In some curious way, the scene, so far down that the people looked like toys, nudged a memory for Jan.

'Let's go down there,' she said suddenly. 'Then I might remember.'

But by the time they reached the harbour her mind was blank again, and Marco a little irritated by the unnecessary journey, the lost time.

'I'm sorry,' she apologised weakly. 'Up there, it seemed almost clear, but now it's gone. Must be all these people.'

His lips curled fastidiously. 'Trippers. A herd for the milking. Now do you see why we don't want Barini to become a popular resort?'

'I see people looking prosperous, Marco. The money flows in. Look at it, walking over the gangways to give itself up.'

He laughed shortly. 'Wait till you see Anacapri!'

'What I've seen so far,' she told him tartly, 'is remarkably beautiful, and frankly I don't see beauty in picturesque dirt and beggars.'

There we go, she despaired. Can't we spend one morning together without quarrelling?

The taxi zigzagged up hairpin bends much steeper and longer than those of Barini. The air was heavy with orange blossom, acacia, and, Jan had to admit, petrol fumes. But after a while their driver turned off into a side road and all the tourist traffic was left behind. When they arrived at their destination Jan drew in a deep breath.

The house was faced in white stucco and pink tiles. Along its arcaded front palm trees grew, and small fountains tossed their silver into the air and fell back into marble basins with a musical splash. It was more regular than the Villa Tramonti, and this formality, among the rioting foliage and flowers of the island, gave it a special beauty. But as they walked across the garden to the great white doors Jan felt a trembling in her stomach. Sheer nerves, she told herself crossly, and what have I to be scared of? If the girl is here, it's between herself and her brother.

A servant conducted them to a shady *salone,* where the young mistress of the house was writing letters at a graceful tulipwood escritoire. She threw down her pen and ran to meet them.

'Marco! How lovely! I was feeling desperate for company. And bless you for bringing Bianca. Darling, we'll have such a talk. You'll let her stay for lunch, Marco? Say you will. You can't be in a hurry —not today!'

Marco bent over her hand, touched his lips to it. 'My delightful Gina, you look more beautiful than ever as a wife. Cesare has robbed all the bachelors of Italy! Look, I've brought you an English girl instead of Bianca. May I present Signorina Jan Lynton, who is my mother's guest?'

'I'm sorry. As you came in through the doors, you

looked so like Bianca. I'm very happy to meet you, Miss Lynton. But what have you done with my dear little bridesmaid?'

'Visiting her aunts in Florence,' said Marco, with a slight downturn of the corners of his mouth. Gina laughed.

'Oh, those aunts! The one with the liver? And the other with her dreadful old spaniel? Poor Bianca!'

She looked at Jan curiously, as if wishing to ask a question but not quite asking it.

'I am taking care of Signora Cellini in Bianca's absence,' Jan told her. 'I have some nursing experience, and am combining a little work with a great deal of holiday.'

Their hostess nodded understandingly. 'What a splendid idea! How is your mamma, Marco? Better, I hope.'

He shrugged expressively. 'Not good, not bad. Today Jan has a day off, and the convent has sent two sisters over to sit with Mamma. So I thought our guest should see something of Capri—and, of course, the best thing in it, your lovely garden and your view.'

'Cesare's grandfather made the garden and God made the view. Will you take coffee first?' Gina's hand hovered over a silver bell. 'Or wine?'

When they refused refreshment, she led them into the garden. 'Not as well cared for as your mother's, Marco. But nobody ever looks at it, poor thing. They look at the view and see no more.'

Jan walked to the low white balcony and stood without speaking. Words were impossible. The whole of the Bay of Naples stretched out before her—the islands, the white boats, the great curve of the peninsula. And Vesuvius, clear for once of heat haze.

'The trouble with Barini,' she heard Marco saying, 'is that we are too far out to see so much. We see the volcano only on the clearest days of winter, and from one point only. Are you sure we are not in your way, Gina? I thought you might have guests.'

'Cesare adores guests. But our last batch left yesterday, and the next lot—my cousins from Milan—are not due till the end of the week. So I have a breathing space to think my own thoughts and talk to you. Tell me, when is the wedding? Bianca will be such a lovely bride. Shall you be here, Miss Lynton, for this famous Cellini wedding?'

She was speaking in fairly good English, so Jan replied in her own language. 'I'm afraid not, *signora*. I shall be back in England long before that.'

The time till lunch passed pleasantly. Gina was only too ready to show the English girl round the villa, of which she was obviously proud. Marco begged permission to stay on the terrace and smoke a cigar, as no doubt there would be dresses to look at, and curtains and carpets to admire. Such feminine things were beyond him.

Bianca isn't here, Jan decided, but all the same he's playing safe. If I go round the house, and he stays in the garden, there'll be no escape route.

'I saw the photograph of your wedding,' she told Gina, following through the long *salone* and admiring the cool white marble floor. 'I thought it the most beautiful dress I've ever seen.'

'But useless, once the wedding is over. I have an idea. Would you like to wear it, for your wedding? No one in England has seen it, but I can't lend it to my friends here, as everyone—but everyone—in Italy saw it in the newspapers.'

Jan flushed deeply. 'I'd love to. But my wedding is a long way away. First one needs a bridegroom.'

'And you haven't one? Oh, my dear, I was so sure you were going to marry our Marco. He has such a proud and possessing look. We've all been waiting years for him to choose, and when I saw him look at you, I said to myself *This is the one!*'

'No,' Jan said in a choked voice. 'Oh no! I'm unsuitable. I mean—not the sort of girl a Cellini would marry. He would never even think of me in that way.'

Gina gave her a penetrating look. 'Have I said something I shouldn't? Are you in love with him?'

'I have a career, madame.'

'I see.' Gina closed the vast wardrobe carefully. 'A career. That is a pity, when you are so attractive and young. You and Marco would make such a fine couple. Well, we shall have to wait a little longer, but when he does marry, all the daughters and mothers we know will sigh with relief. The strain is terrible, believe me!' She laughed lightly and changed the subject. 'Marco says his mother is not bad, not good. What does that mean, exactly?'

'It means she needs her daughter. She misses Bianca terribly. You will know how forgetful the poor soul is? Well, I think sometimes she is afraid Bianca is gone for ever, like her husband.'

'But she believes her husband is alive, in another room.'

'She pretends she believes. Sometimes she knows quite well he is dead. But she is terribly and secretly afraid about Bianca.'

'Doesn't Bianca write, or telephone? Marco must tell her she must.'

Jan shrugged. 'The young are careless about writing. They don't know how the older generation wait and watch and worry, if letters do not come.'

'You speak as if you are old yourself. You shouldn't do that.'

'I've nursed old people. I've had to tell them, morning after morning, the letter hasn't come. I've seen the tears wiped away secretly, the hopeful smile fade.

Believe me, I know what I'm talking about. I'm young too, but I take good care to write to my parents every week, wherever I am. I couldn't bear to see that look on their faces.'

'You love people, *signorina*. You have great sympathy and warmth. One day you'll give all that to one man, and he will be fortunate. I am sad that it is not my dear Marco, after all. Well, let us go back to him, or he'll think we've forgotten him.' She gave Jan a long penetrating look. 'As if anyone could forget Marco, eh? He is not easily forgotten, that one.'

Jan followed Gina back to the terrace, where Marco had settled himself for a long wait. Chair tilted back, his feet one on another, his white panama hat tipped over his eyes, he looked the picture of a man relaxed, content, and patiently waiting till the womenfolk should choose to come back.

'Up, lazybones,' cried Gina. 'You said you'd promised to take this girl to Anacapri to look at the shops. And you must buy her an expensive, lovely present there, for a memorial of her visit.'

'Memento,' Jan corrected, laughing. 'A memorial is for when you're dead. We have a prettier, older word which is rarely used now. A keepsake.'

Gina tilted her head, eyebrows drawn together in query. 'Ah—I know. Keep it for my sake? That's a good word and I shall remember to use it. Thank you. Do you hear, Marco? Buy her a keepsake.'

'I intend to. She must choose something she likes.'

'That's no good. Politeness will make her choose something cheap, and you ought to buy her something splendid. Walk along to the villa of San Michele— Jan must see all the little shops there. I may say Jan? On the right there is a shop where they have beautiful kaftans—and shoes. We are famous for our shoes if you buy them from the man who makes them. Not the tourist stuff, but the real thing.'

Marco kissed her hand. 'I'll remember. Thank you for lunch, and for your kindness, Gina. Give my regards to Cesare. I'm sorry to have missed him, but no doubt we'll meet in Rome before long.'

On the rest of the short journey to Anacapri, Jan's mind was in turmoil. Gina's words about Marco had come right out of the blue, left her shaken and incredulous. She felt desperately empty inside, drained of emotion. If only she had had a moment to prepare herself for the shock of hearing those lightly spoken words! As it was, she was terribly afraid she had betrayed herself, and went hot and cold with embarrassment and shame.

Would there come a time when Gina's laughing voice would say *Of course that little nurse person adored you, Marco. Didn't you know? I hope you bought her a nice present to console her for losing the love of her life.*

Marco, too, was silent, his eyes on the twisting road rising so steeply to the summit of the island which itself was no more than a rock flung into the sea by some giant of legend.

' Bianca hadn't been there,' he said when the hairpin straightened for a short stretch. ' Gina was genuine, don't you agree? No artifice about her. She always says what she thinks, straight out. You didn't see any trace?'

' No. I told her how much your mother missed Bianca. If they are in touch, that message will get back. Apart from that, we talked of—other things. She offered to lend me her wedding dress.'

' What did our cool career girl say to that?'

' That I was a career girl, of course.'

He made an impatient exclamation. ' Some day, my dear Jan, one man will light a fire in you that will consume without destroying you. No woman is as cool as you make believe you are.'

The fire was already alight, burning, consuming. It was false that it would not destroy her. What could have been a glory like the sun might shrivel her into a bitter old maid if she was not terribly careful to keep bitterness out of the loss. She did not answer but sat stiff, her mouth dry, her heart sick. Her love for Marco possessed her completely. Gina's careless words had torn her protective skin aside, left bare the throbbing pain.

She was thankful when they reached Anacapri. It was a relief to get out of the taxi, walk among the bright crowd of holidaymakers, admire the endless selection of shoes and scarves, smart dresses and elegant leatherware offered for sale—the pottery, the mosaics, marquetry, fine silks and delicate cottons. Up here, they catered for the more affluent visitor. A tea-room offered *English Tea and Toast*. Toast, Marco said, was a legacy from the travelling English of Edwardian days, like tea. Nowhere in Europe do they make it so well.

He took her to a shoemaker and made her choose style and colour. 'Your shoes will arrive all in good time, and will fit as perfectly as your skin. Now we'll find that kaftan.'

By the side of the big modern store crammed with luxury goods, he showed her a narrow lane, lined with tiny shops displaying everything from straw sandals to silken tunics, exquisite marquetry, statuettes, wood-carvings. The lane was rarely wider than six feet, the wares flowed out of the shops on to tables and stools. When they came to the dealer in rainbow-coloured silks, Marco stopped and studied the display intently.

'That one,' he said at last, pointing to a full-length robe with long sleeves in sea-green silk edged with silver. 'It's the colour of your eyes when you look at the sea. I'd like to think of you wearing it.'

'*Bellissima!*' exclaimed the stout salesman, kissing the tips of his podgy fingers. His wife, drawn into the conference by his raptures, nodded vigorously. The woman had, Jan reflected, probably never worn anything more exciting than her present black skirt and high-necked cotton blouse, but there was a shrewd approval in her chocolate-brown eyes. She waddled back into the tiny shop and brought out a long looking-glass.

'No need even for that,' Marco declared. 'I approve and that is enough. Jan, have the goodness to walk away and let me haggle with this daylight robber. Not that I begrudge you the price he is asking, but he shouldn't be allowed to get away with it.'

Obediently she slipped her arms out of the lovely thing, picked up her bag and walked away to the next display. The sounds of the harangue rose and fell. What a true Italian Marco was, she thought with an amused smile. He could most likely buy out the man and all his stock and shop too, but could not resist the chance of a friendly haggle in which both sides would finally emerge completely satisfied.

When he rejoined her and handed over the pink paper bag containing her kaftan, she teased him gently, 'You look like a cat which has eaten the cream. I suppose you robbed that poor man of the bread from his children's mouths?'

'So he assured me. What next?'

'Presents for my parents, and some of my friends. If you don't care to be seen shopping on my price level, I'll pretend I'm not with you.'

'On the contrary! I shall enjoy it. I shall see you are not cheated, and help you drive a hard bargain. You will never know the real joy of shopping until you learn to haggle.'

'Isn't it dreadfully time-wasting?'

He shrugged. 'What is time? We have all the time there is. It is as interesting to be concerned over a hundred lire as over a million.'

'Take care of the pence and the pounds will take care of themselves?'

'A wise observation, *signorina*. I must remember it. My English has improved, I think.'

'It's a proverb, but long ago fallen into oblivion, I fancy. Look—if I could buy my mother one of those pretty shopping baskets, we could put everything else into it. The one embroidered with shells?'

Marco examined the basket she chose, and dismissed it. 'We must find a handmade one, with leather handles. It will cost a little more but last for years and look more elegant. Follow me!'

He was now the dedicated shopper. Jan followed him, laughing, in and out of shops; mulled over stalls, rejected, accepted, and haggled, at his direction. Eventually she decided she had bought enough, and he carried her off to the flower-decked restaurant terrace where *English Tea and Toast* was advertised as a speciality.

'Satisfied?' he smiled.

'Very satisfied indeed. You'd make a good housewife.'

'The trick is,' he said, buttering toast liberally, 'to pick out the locally made stuff from the imported tourist rubbish. Jan, I believe you know where Bianca is.'

She could not believe her ears. '*What* did you say?'

'You do, don't you? This morning I wasn't sure, but I've been watching you all day. I'm a pretty shrewd businessman, my dear, and one learns to know faces. The flick of an eyelash, the twist of a lip— sometimes one's survival in business depends on knowing the significance of such things. Like a sailor's survival depends on the feel of the weather. Yesterday you knew nothing. Today you are different. You have learned something. Was it from Gina, when you were alone with her?'

'No. We hardly mentioned her name. We spoke of the house, the furniture, Gina's wedding dress, Signora Cellini.'

His eyebrows rose. 'Then why are you blushing crimson? You are not the blushing kind, are you? What else did you talk of?'

She said furiously, 'You have no right to question me like that. This is not the Inquisition. We've been so happy together all day, I thought we were friends. And now it seems you have been suspecting me, watching me down to the flick of an eyelash. It's horrible!'

Guilt made her angry, but with herself, not him. Now she was really in a trap, compelled to lie to Marco who had been so good to her; or to break her promise to a stranger who might or might not be genuine.

'Suspecting isn't the word I'd have used. I don't suspect—I know. You are keeping a secret from me; possibly a secret you don't even know you possess. All day I've hoped you would tell me. Now I am compelled to ask.'

'But I am not compelled to answer. I don't know where Bianca is, and I learned nothing from Gina about her. In fact, she spoke mostly of you. She said you were an eligible bachelor, that when you finally married it would be a great occasion, and that speculation among the young unmarried and their mothers was a strain.'

He laughed at that. 'Is that all? Poor Gina! Have you noticed how newly-married people always try to marry off all their friends? Nothing more?'

'If you are asking if I'm keeping a secret from you, I am. But you will learn it all in good time. Not from me. It is not mine to tell.'

The magic of the day was gone. She was suddenly aware of the garishness of the colours, the overcrowded piazza, the thrusting coach-parties, the peeling paint and shabbiness behind the advertisements. A moment of disenchantment, the fairy gold turning into a handful of dried leaves.

'You are entitled to keep your own counsel, naturally. But I still think you may have learned something without realising that it is important. Couldn't we explore the possibility of that?' He was keeping a tight control of his voice; his manner remained as charming as before, yet the easy atmosphere was gone. He was the head of his house again, the head of a vast business empire and no longer in holiday mood. He had waited and pounced, and had her in his trap.

'One thing,' she remembered suddenly, 'which puzzled me, and I may have had it in the back of my mind all day. A trouser suit of Bianca's has vanished from her wardrobe.'

'Stolen? One of the maids? Francesca is honest, but her family are lazy good-for-nothings. She supports them, I believe. A dozen or more mouths to feed, poor child. I won't have thieves in my house. We shall have to investigate.'

She put her hand on his, as it lay on the table. 'No, Marco, say nothing. Wait and see what happens. Bianca took very little when she went. She'll be in need of fresh clothes by this time.'

'She came home and took it? And no one saw?'

'I've been wondering. Suppose she's on the island still?'

He frowned. 'Who would dare shelter her?'

She had used those very words herself, when speaking to Paolo. In Marco's mouth they sounded impossibly feudal, and her hackles rose. 'Stop talking as if you owned the island and everybody on it, body and soul! You don't. And if you did you'd need to be ashamed of yourself, for the poverty, the dirt, and bad housing. You're not lord of all you survey, so some people might hide her for the sake of reminding the Cellinis that they are not all-powerful. You can't be popular with everyone, Marco, if you hold mediaeval ideas. You may have succeeded in keeping prosperity out of the island in order to preserve your own Shangri-la, but you can't keep ideas out.'

His face became a polite mask, tight-lipped, cold of eye.

'I have searched the island,' he said distantly. 'As you know. So has Dino, and he knows more hiding places than I ever could. You don't think—'

She saw the question written on his face and answered it before he could ask. 'No, I don't think Dino has hidden her. He's probably one of the people who wouldn't dare. Besides, he likes you.'

He pushed back his chair. 'Speaking of Dino, we should be making for the harbour. He will come early, as always, so if you've finished your shopping we could be on our way. He'll have to take the nuns back to Sorrento later, and the Mother Superior does not like them to be late.'

She collected her things and stood up. The treat was over. She had offended, and was to be taken home early like a naughty child.

Signora Cellini had had a happy day, she said. She was well, and had slept during the siesta hour. The nuns sat side by side placidly, hands folded in their laps, waiting till it should please someone to take them home to their convent. Gently, with polite smiles, they refused an invitation to remain for dinner.

Marco himself drove them down to the harbour. Jan unwrapped the kaftan for Signora Cellini to see, then went to change. It would not do to add to her crimes by keeping the master of the house waiting for his evening meal.

The blue trouser suit was back. Jan rang for Francesca.

'Si, si, signorina. You made a mistake. See, it was

hanging at the other end of the wardrobe, next to the bridesmaid's dress. Look how the folds of the long skirt hid it.'

'When did the Signorina Bianca bring it back, Francesca? Today, when we were out?'

The girl paled. Her hands, outstretched in protest, trembled. 'I have not seen her—I swear it.'

Jan looked at the terrified girl in exasperated silence. Suddenly she felt sick to death of the whole Cellini set-up. What did it matter to her where Bianca had chosen to hide herself? Why should she bully this poor child, so easily scared out of her wits, in order to pull the Cellini irons out of the fire? How much more peaceful life would have been, now and in the future, if she had never set eyes on Marco, the villa, everything.

'Go away,' she told Francesca. 'It doesn't matter. I made a mistake. I'm sorry. Please don't cry any more.'

'You believe me, that I have not seen Signorina Bianca?'

Oddly enough, Jan discovered, she did believe the girl. If Bianca had slipped in during the day, Francesca had not seen her. Three years' hospital training helped one to hear the ring of truth in a desperate voice. She nodded, and the girl scurried off.

Three years' training also taught one to observe accurately. Not to miss the smallest detail. How could she have missed that trouser suit on the rail, when she had searched for it so carefully?

Dinner was easy, after all. Signora Cellini had had a happy day. She was animated, full of chatter about her friends the nuns and eager to hear news of Gina and Cesare. Jan was made to describe the house, the furniture, Gina's clothes, in detail.

Marco put in a word occasionally, but his mood was remote and calm. Far different from Jan's own chaotic emotions, which she found difficult to analyse.

Impatience to be done with the villa and all its devious ways; a longing to be safe within the walls of the hospital, secure in the familiar routine, part of the vast throbbing life within the great glass walls. A bitter longing to remain here, within sight and sound of Marco Cellini, whom she hated and loved in equal measure.

If time would stand still—here and now!

Tomorrow her promise to Paolo ended. She would tell Marco all she knew. And the next day she would go home and it would all be over. A dream—fading with the coming of day, as dreams do.

The Signora lingered long after her usual time for retiring, talking happily. Then she begged Jan to bring out her guitar and sing. Jan glanced enquiringly at Marco, who nodded.

She plucked the strings experimentally, then began with some modern folk music, singing softly. The Mediterranean night deepened from violet to purple, the stars came out one by one; the flower scent which would be her longest-lasting memory of the Villa Tramonti hung heavy about them, mingled with the smell of Marco's cigar. After a while he left the two women, and stood at a distance staring down over the terrace to the sea and the headland far below. Was he listening? She thought not. He seemed lost in thought. Lost to me for ever, she thought as she sang.

Her mouth curved into a wry smile. How can one lose what one has never possessed?

At last the Signora said she was tired. Jan put the instrument away and gave the elderly woman her arm. Marco came back to them and kissed his mama goodnight.

'Goodnight, my son. You are kind to your old mother, God bless you. It has been a happy, happy day. You, and my dear Jan, and Bianca.'

Jan's heart turned over. So the girl had been here!

But Marco took the words coolly.

'Did she stay for tea—Bianca?'

'Why, of course, dear. This is her home, why shouldn't she? You know Bianca loves her English tea as much as I do.'

'Did the nuns have tea too?'

A frown drew the elegant, delicate brows together. 'Nuns, dear? What nuns?'

Jan caught the man's light, unhappy sigh. Living on the narrow edge between the real and the unreal, how hard it must be for him.

The Signora took a long time to settle. She fussed gently over this and that, but at last her sleeping tablet took effect and she drifted into light sleep.

Jan had been with her a whole hour. Marco must have gone long ago, to his own rooms somewhere in the heart of the villa.

CHAPTER VII

'Come here, Jan.'

Marco spoke out of the darkness. At first, coming out of the lamplight of the house, Jan could not see him.

'I'm here, on the terrace wall. I want to talk to you.'

As she moved towards him, he held out his hand for hers, drew her towards him. Side by side, they looked out across the water. He pointed to moving lights at sea. 'Fishing boats. Jan, can you really leave us? Leave all this? I have been thinking that in little more than thirty-six hours, you will be gone. Please stay, Jan *cara mia*! We need you here.'

His voice was soft and deep, dangerously tempting. If he meant to exert all his charm to persuade her to stay, it would be so difficult to say no. Yet go she must. Nothing else was possible. Did he know, could he suspect, how his persuasions would tear her heart?

'Holidays come to an end,' she forced herself to speak lightly. 'It is always sad. And then, after all, one is happy to be home again. It happens every year, Marco. Even when I was a child and went to Bridlington with a bucket and spade, I yelled all the way to the station. And next day I was playing with the kids next door quite happily.'

'Do we mean so little to you? You will forget us, in a single day?'

Not in a lifetime! She moistened dry lips and said smiling, 'You've given me a wonderful holiday and I shall remember you all for a long time. I only wish I'd brought a camera, so I could show everyone what the villa looks like. You've reminded me that I should be packing, Marco. I ought to say goodnight, and thank you for a splendid day on Capri. The Blue Grotto and—'

He closed her mouth with a long, hard kiss. She felt the beat of his heart as her body relaxed against his. This was irresistible magic. The moonlight, the heady scents, the physical dominance of an utterly fascinating man. Slowly, her arms slid round his neck, and she gave her mouth to his.

After a long time, he released her. She was trembling with joy, completely relaxed, completely happy. There will be this to remember, her heart sang. Marco's kisses were like champagne in her blood. But thrilling though it was, she felt a warning touch her like an icy finger.

Marco was not a boy, to be carried away by the urge of the body, the enchantment of night and music. He did nothing without calculation. So what did he want of her?

She did not dare to think that his embraces meant more than a momentary emotion sparked off by the thought of her imminent departure, a sudden physical urge born of the long day together, the sad yearning songs she had been singing; and perhaps of a sudden rejection, like her own, of worry and responsibility and anxiety. He was young too, and he had suffered much, these last days.

'You see?' he said, almost laughing with triumph. 'You cannot resist me.'

'Who could?' she murmured, yielding to the pressure of his arm around her shoulder. 'You really are a fascinating creature when you try, Marco Cellini. And I am as susceptible to Italian enchantment as any other woman.'

'So you will not refuse to stay?' He drew her close, found the tender spot below her ear and put his lips to it. His breath was in her hair. 'You will stay with us, *cara mia?*'

So he was only coaxing, like a child, with kisses! He could be a baby too, if he did not get his own way. She had known his granite hardness, the quickness of his Latin temper. Now he was trying the other way, the gentle approach.

Her soft laughter made him laugh too, and grumble. 'You are laughing at me?'

'Of course I'm laughing at you. Don't imagine all these kisses deceive me for a moment. You choose the time and place so perfectly.'

His lips in her hair, he whispered, 'You are not angry?'

'Not angry at all.' She turned her face to his, to meet his mouth. 'Do I seem angry, in your arms and kissing you?'

'So you are not leaving the day after tomorrow?'

She drew away, and taking his face between her palms, looked into his eyes. 'Listen, Marco Cellini. We've had a lovely day, you've held me, kissed me— and I've kissed you. And we've both enjoyed every minute of it. But that makes no difference to tomorrow and the day after. This is tonight. This is Italian magic—an hour to remember, an hour out of time. It has nothing to do with reality.'

He gripped her wrists tightly. She could see the gleam in his eyes, the firm line of cheek and chin.

'It has everything to do with reality. It makes all the difference to today and tomorrow. I am asking you to marry me, *cara mia*.'

Stunned with surprise, Jan could neither move nor speak. She felt a cool breath of air from the sea on her bare arms, a chill of regret that the minutes of their closeness were over so soon. But where she should have felt elation, joy, fantastic happiness, she experienced only a dull anger.

So he was prepared to go as far as that, to keep her for his mother? It would solve his problem so neatly, would it not? One day soon, his sister Bianca would marry, go off to her husband's home. And that would leave a problem on Marco's plate. The beautiful Signora Cellini, mentally unbalanced after the tragic death of her husband, needing care and privacy. He would never be able to take her to his Roman apartment, for how could she live her gentle, harmless life out there? How could he, so proud, so touchy, ever allow his friends and acquaintances to know how unbalanced his mother was?

But an English nurse, who knew nobody in Italy and could not, therefore, gossip? What a splendid solution, leaving Marco to live his life free of worries!

A marriage without love. A marriage of convenience. *His* convenience.

The thoughts raced round and round in her mind for what seemed a long time.

' Jan?' His voice—that velvety voice full of enchantment—was asking her for the response she could not give.

She shivered in the wind off the sea. Why was it so cold suddenly? She pressed her hands over her eyes a moment.

' No, Marco. Don't you see, you are asking the impossible?'

' Why impossible? If you mean, I haven't approached your family, I can do that. As you see, I'm not a poor man, Jan. You like Italy, you could be happy here. There is much you could do on the island, as my wife. I admit I've neglected it. So did my father. He had other interests, and so have I. But you—so full of ideas—'

That too? She was to be his conscience on the island. Stay here, as isolated as in a convent, play the great lady and look after his tenants, while he—? *What* other interests?

' Please stop, Marco. I've said I won't marry you,

and that's the end. You had no right to ask me, in this way. You're not the only one who has other interests. Have you forgotten I have a career?'

As if that would have mattered, if he had said *Jan, I love you!*

He brushed his hand across his forehead. 'I do not understand this *career*. What is it, but nursing the sick? Is that enough for a woman, for her whole life? Don't you want marriage, a home, children and grand-children around you? What sort of a woman are you, Jan? I thought I knew you. I thought when you kissed me so passionately just now—yes, you did—I felt the warmth of a real woman. But you are still so cold, so dedicated. How can I reach you?'

'Not by offering bribes,' she said coldly. She had not known she could be so angry. So she was to pro-vide him with the children every Italian coveted? No doubt to an Italian girl in her position, the marriage he offered would be irresistible. Money, a splendid villa, children, a fine estate. And a husband who conveniently lived in Rome and did not bother her too much. But it was not Jan's own idea of what a mar-riage should be, and she could never be content with second-best.

'I'm sorry, Marco,' she said again, to his silence.

As he moved away from her, the moonlight fell full on his face, and she felt a surge of wild hope as she saw disappointment there, which was almost longing. His hands came out to her, but did not reach her. Pride came into his face, something of anger, some-thing of the patrician reserve which was so typically Cellini. His hands dropped. For him, an episode had ended. That was plain to see.

'Now I know you are not a real woman. When I offer you everything a woman is supposed to want, you call it a bribe. What sort of talk is that? Is my name nothing? My family? Can I offer you no position in

Italian society, no proper home? Do English girls think of these things as bribes? Well, I shall offer no more bribes. If I am so undesirable that I have to offer bribes to get a woman to marry me, I shall remain a bachelor for ever. Any man has his pride, and I shall keep mine.'

She started towards him. 'No, oh no, Marco! I didn't mean you were unattractive, nor that your name and family meant nothing. Oh dear, I've handled this so badly, and been so unkind and tactless. Please believe me, I didn't mean to hurt your pride so deeply. I'm honoured, greatly honoured, by your offer of marriage. I'm not even worthy of it, as far as money or family are concerned. We're just ordinary, everyday people. I've no long pedigree or fortune, and I'm sure I'd have no dowry or anything like that. What I meant was something different. I—I can't do what you wish, that's all.'

There was a long moment of silence. Then he bowed formally, turned and marched stiffly away. Jan, alone on the terrace, shivered with cold. She should go indoors and get warm, yet she was too disturbed in her mind to move.

It was to this terrace he had brought her on the first day. Together, they had stood on this very spot, looking down at the sea, the headland, the old stone castle. Every day since then, her feeling for him had grown and grown. That he would ever propose had been beyond her wildest dreams. That she would refuse him would have seemed absurd.

Yet she had done so, and sent him marching away stiff with rage and wounded pride. One thing was certain—he would never give her a second chance.

If he had loved her, how different this moment would have been. But she could not marry on his terms. She wanted her marriage to be loving, sharing, giving each to the other, in trust and tenderness. None

135

of the things he considered important really mattered. Not to her, though it was obvious they mattered tremendously to him.

What would have happened to her, when and if he found the right kind of woman for his wife? His own countrywoman, rich and influential, of good family and estate. What of the little English nurse then? Or when his mother died, as in the course of time must happen—what then, when he had no more need of her?

She had been right—right—to refuse him. But the loneliness rushing in on her, the emptiness, the sense of life to be endured without hope, was too much to bear. She buried her face in her hands and gave way to the dreadful grief which shook her.

When the storm was over, she wiped the blinding tears away. She must go indoors, her flesh was cold as marble. But she could not resist one last look over the terrace to the moonlit path across the sea. And a light went out. The whole coast below her was now lost in velvet blackness. Yet a minute before, there had been a light. Where? Surely in the castle?

She knew, with absolute certainty, where Bianca was.

That was the knowledge which had been nagging at the back of her mind for days. On that first day, Marco had pointed out the castle, told her Bianca's godfather lived there. Asked her to wave if the old man waved to her.

She had never done so. Why?

Because he had never waved to her. And he had not done so, because Bianca, his beloved goddaughter, was down there with him. So why should he wave to an unknown figure on a balcony?

As she crawled, shivering, into bed, she examined the idea carefully. Why had not Marco asked at the castle? Perhaps he had done so, and been told a lie. What if the old man didn't even know the girl was under his roof? It looked to be a big, rambling place where half an army could lie concealed—so why not one girl?

What if the Signora had told the truth about taking tea with her daughter? Why not? She wasn't wrong all the time. If Bianca had an ally in the Villa Tramonti, she could find out when the coast was clear and slip in to visit her mother. Someone had warned her, too, that the blue trouser suit had been missed. Francesca, without a doubt.

Bianca must be fetched home, not later than tomorrow. Because tomorrow she, Jan, had sworn to tell Marco the truth about Paolo. And Paolo, if he was anything of a man, would arrive at the villa to announce that he loved Bianca, and to demand her hand in marriage.

There would be fireworks. Bianca, cause of all the trouble, must be there with Paolo.

Jan woke early. Today would be horrible, full of trouble. But at least Marco's attention would be fully occupied, and she herself could tactfully keep out of the way. Most probably Paolo and Bianca would be marched into Marco's study and interviewed there, in decent privacy and out of earshot of the servants.

She would have to fetch Bianca herself, that much was obvious. She could not let the girl walk into trouble unprepared; nor let her remain down there, oblivious of what was happening at the Villa Tramonti. She did not doubt for a moment, even now in the light of day, that the castle was Bianca's hiding place.

She rang for Francesca and before she was out of the shower the girl was there. The child looked dark-eyed and harassed, as if she had cried a good deal lately.

' Please bring my breakfast in here. I won't eat out of doors this morning. And Francesca—'

Startled eyes flicked a glance up at Jan, then the lids

lowered. '*Si, signorina?*'

'After breakfast I am going down to the castle. Is there a path down the cliff?'

'The castle? Oh no, *signorina*. The cliff path is terribly dangerous. You could fall and break your neck, or go straight down into the sea.'

'Is there another way?'

'By the road.'

'That is too far.'

The girl nodded in agreement, and pleated her apron. 'Why are you going, *signorina*?'

'I think you know. I am going to fetch the Signorina Bianca home.'

The dark eyes, huge in the pale face, opened wide. 'Does—does the Signore know?'

'No. And I shall never tell him, Francesca, so you can tell me if you helped. You did, I think.'

'Not me. But I knew about it. She and her brother, they quarrelled terribly. They have the Cellini temper, both of them. We, the servants that is, felt sorry for the girl—well, the younger ones did, because we know what it is like, to be in love, and we had seen her meeting the beautiful young man on the beach. But the older ones, Maria-Teresa and old Guido, wanted to tell the master. They said he was right, and that she should marry the man she was betrothed to.'

'So what happened?'

The girl shrugged expressively. 'She ran away. Only to make the Signore understand she was serious— and only for a little time. But now—we are frightened, *signorina*. It made a difference, your coming. We never expected you.'

'What sort of difference?'

'The Signore could save his pride. We knew, when we saw you wearing her things, that he meant us to believe his sister was here. Not the servants, of course, but the people on the island. His kind of people.'

'So what do we do now, Francesca? I have to go home to England tomorrow. The Signora will be alone. Bianca is needed now. Are you going to help me fetch her home, or not?'

The Italian girl bobbed a funny little curtsey. 'I will bring your breakfast, and I will ask downstairs what is to be done. You swear you will not tell?'

'I have already sworn it.'

Left alone, Jan finished dressing and filled in the time by doing some of her packing. She needed to keep her hands occupied, to prevent herself thinking too much about last night.

The whole thing seemed too impossible to be real. Had she been in his arms, kissed and kissing; feeling the beat of his heart close to her, feeling his breath in her hair, hearing the soft murmur of his voice?

Could it be true that she had refused to marry the man she loved? And in such terms as would make it certain that she was never given a second chance?

I'm crazy, she thought. Stark, raving mad. Life is tough for a girl on her own. I'll never marry anyone else—and even if I did, what sort of life would it be? Struggle all the time. Finding a house, getting a crippling mortgage, bringing up children in to-day's tough world. People do it, and survive, even enjoy it, but it isn't easy. Two weeks in a villa like this would be the fulfilment of a lifetime's dream for any of the young marrieds I know.

And I could have had all this, and Marco too. The rich life of big cars, yachts, travel, clothes bought on the Via Veneto. He's generous, he'd have denied me nothing material. Given me a free hand to make a few improvements on this island, asked little besides looking after his mother, whom I love anyway.

And bearing his children. He had not meant his marriage of convenience to be lacking in any of the marital duties. Who knows, in time he might have come to love me?

She snapped the locks of her suitcase. No regrets, Jan Lynton, she told herself sternly. There is only one sort of marriage, and that is to marry the man you love because he loves you. And if I can't have that sort, I'll have none. Nursing is a good career and women don't have to marry nowadays, in order to live a full and satisfying life. So that's that.

Just then Francesca came back with the breakfast tray. A tall glass of frosted orange juice, hot coffee and a big jug of cream, and rolls piping hot from Maria-Teresa's oven.

'There is a donkey, *signorina*. It knows the way down to the road and is sure-footed. My little brother Pedro is here. He brings the fish. He will show you.'

A donkey! Jan caught Francesca's eye and laughed. After a moment's hesitation the girl laughed too.

'But it is a very nice donkey, *signorina*. Better than walking. Pedro will wait and bring you back. Or if the Signore does not want the beach-buggy, Dino will come and collect you.'

'What? Is Dino in this too?'

'But of course. We all are.'

'Dino is supposed to have searched the whole island.'

The eyes were merry now. 'He did. But he could not search inside the castle, could he?'

Jan put on an expression she hoped was a true copy of Sister Tutor's. 'What is the Signore going to say to you all, when he learns all about the tricks you've been up to?'

'*Signorina*! You promised!'

'He won't learn from me. But he is a remarkable man, Francesca. Don't be too sure he will not find out, some day. I wouldn't like him to be truly angry with me. Aren't you scared?'

The girl bit her lip and studied the polished floor. 'Yes, I am. He will find out—he always does. He will tell my father to beat me. But the Signorina Bianca will pay me well, so I shan't mind the beating. The money will go towards my marriage.'

'Who shall you marry? Do you have someone?'

'My father hasn't decided yet.'

'Is there someone special you'd like your father to choose?'

'Oh, yes, yes, there is. His name is Filiberto, but his parents own a *ristorante* down on the harbour side, so he would need a good dowry, and my father has so many children. It is difficult, *signorina*, for a girl like me. My money is needed at home.'

'Surely Signor Cellini would help with a dowry?' Jan thought how little the money would mean to Marco, how vast the amount must seem to plump little Francesca. 'Why don't you speak to the Signora about it?'

The girl blushed crimson. 'But I dare not. Besides, he will be so angry when he finds out what I have done that he may send me away and I shall have no work and no wages for a long time. There is much unemployment on the island.'

'But why do you allow all this to happen? You're too old to be beaten, and there must be plenty of employment on Capri or in Naples.'

'Naples? That nest of robbers! I wouldn't go there for a million lire. But Capri—I never thought of going to Capri. What could I do?'

'What you do here. Or you could come to England. Do you know, people in England would pay almost anything you cared to ask, for the sort of help you give here in the villa? In a year, you'd save enough for a good dowry.'

The girl drew in a deep, excited breath. 'You would take me?'

'No. You must think about it first. Don't do anything in a hurry. But if you decide to come, I will help all I can. See, I'll leave you my address. Now, where's this famous donkey of yours?'

'Wait! No one must see you go. I'll look round the terrace to see where the Signore is.'

In the few moments the girl was gone, Jan had time to regret her impulsive invitation to England. Francesca would be happier here, unspoilt and with her own people around her. She was too young, too innocent of life, to survive the rough and tumble of a big city. If she found work, it would have to be in some quiet country place, or by the sea. There are flowers which will not transplant happily.

Was it true that Marco would tell her father to beat her? Perhaps it was part of the feudal way of life which seemed to obtain in Barini. And if so, did that not also include providing a dowry for the girl too?

If only I could see her happy with her Filiberto, Jan thought regretfully. It was so easy to put aside a pretty nightdress and the Indian slippers Francesca admired. But someone ought to see about her future, or she'd be at the mercy of that work-shy father of hers.

The girl reported that Marco Cellini was working in his study, and led Jan towards the kitchen quarters of the villa, where she had never set foot before. Here, things were very different. The kitchen was dark, untidy, and seemed to be full of people all talking at once. Strings of onions hung from hooks in the plastered walls; the huge kitchen table was piled high with food—chickens, baskets of tomatoes, aubergines gleaming purple. A generous red enamel coffee pot stood among all this richness, from which Maria-Teresa, the cook, dispensed hospitality to all and sundry. It looked, Jan decided, like an enormous oil-painting by one of those old masters, and ought to be hanging on the walls of a gallery, garlic smells and all.

Maria-Teresa was rolling pasta on a cleared space—for ravioli, she called out to Jan in a dialect so strong that Jan could hardly understand. Who on earth were all these people? Surely the villa did not have so many on the staff?

Francesca pulled out little Pietro from the crowd. He was up to his ears in melon, and grinned up at Jan with sticky lips. His eyes twinkled like bright buttons. 'My nephew,' Maria-Teresa introduced with a flourish of her rolling-pin. 'And that is my aunt, in the corner. She brings the lemons, and oranges. She needs coffee, poor soul, after the long walk.'

Jan understood. The villa staff were feeding most of their friends and relations at Marco's expense. Tramonti had long lacked a real mistress, Bianca being too young and untrained, and the Signora so vague and unaware.

The brown donkey was so small, its legs so thin, that Jan hesitated to mount. But Pietro slung a scarlet cushion over the wooden saddle and patted it invitingly. So Jan hoisted herself up, and Pietro dragged the animal into movement by a rope.

It was a steep path down to sea-level, but not as dangerous as Francesca had at first pretended. Jan was content to jog down in a leisurely way, under the shade of shrubby trees whose names she did not know; through tangles of herb-scented weeds that sometimes scratched her dangling legs. Far below the brilliant sea appeared and disappeared between the twisted trees like a mosaic bright with diamond patches of sunlight. Green lizards flicked into crevices as they passed, and iridescent insects came and went like winged jewels.

It was not easy to keep one's seat with the donkey picking its way down the broken path, stumbling sometimes and always with its hind legs well above the level of its forelegs. When, in addition, it put its head down unexpectedly to crop some favourite plant, Jan was in imminent danger of sliding forward over the creature's pretty head. She was thankful when at last they reached the road, reasonably near the castle entrance.

'I'll walk now, Pietro.' She slid off, and stamped a few paces to ease aching muscles. 'Why don't you ride?' She gestured to the saddle, not sure whether it was lack of understanding or shyness which had kept the boy so quiet this far. But Pietro shook his head, preferring to walk and haul the donkey along behind him. His bare brown feet had suffered no damage on the rocky, thistle-strewn descent.

Jan now became concerned about how she was going to get into the castle. Castles, she had often noticed, did not seem to have front doors, and bells which a visitor could ring for admittance. They had moats, and a portcullis; or huge grey-weathered doors big enough to admit an army and studded with iron bolts; chains, and metal spikes. Admittance, in her experience so far, was gained by paying at the entrance. But this was a private castle, lived in by an elderly owner who might not welcome visitors at any time.

She was worried, too, about her appearance. She was hot, dusty, and untidy after the ride. To pay such a call as she intended, one should arrive cool, soignée, and dignified. *Looking like somebody*, her mother would have called it. Jan was only too well aware she was going to arrive at the castle looking like nobody at all.

On the way they passed two women, balancing flat bundles on their heads, and swaying gracefully as they walked. Both had a word for the little boy, who was vocal enough in reply. Then, to Jan's enormous delight, came a wooden cart laden with oranges, drawn by a yoke of two white oxen.

And then the castle.

'Wait for me,' she impressed on the boy. To make sure of her return transport, she showed him a five-hundred-lire note, promising him it when she returned. She guessed the amount, small as it was, to be larger than anything Pietro had had for himself in his whole short life. By the brightness of his chocolate eyes, she knew he would wait for it.

Now for the castle. It dated from the Crusades, so she had been told, and staring up now at the high stone walls, the narrow barred windows, the cruel battlements, she could well imagine it occupied by armed men, caparisoned horses, and all the panoply and glitter of mediaeval warfare. How many prisoners had died in its dungeons, or eaten their hearts out in long imprisonment behind its ramparts?

Entry was not, after all, difficult. The low archway cut through the walls, which were at that point ten feet thick—maybe more, she thought—led into a sunny courtyard round which the inhabited portions of the castle formed a hollow square. There was a well in the middle, in the shadow of which a great white dog slept. A few hens picked about the cobblestones, and a man crossing the yard glanced across, put down a bucket he was carrying, and came to greet her.

' *Per favore*, I should like to speak with the Signorina Bianca Cellini,' Jan said in her best Italian, and with less confidence than she displayed outwardly. The fingers of her right hand were crossed. What if the man said no such person was in the castle? Well, what? A wasted journey, no more. He couldn't eat her. The dog had stirred and now came towards her, but sank into a sitting position at a word from the man, who invited Jan to follow him.

He led her into what she knew must be the great hall, a high chamber the full height of the castle, with a splendid roof of king-post trusses, gilded and painted. The walls were whitewashed and decorated with coats of arms in heraldic colours; scarlet and gold, royal blue and white. Above each escutcheon hung faded and tattered banners, centuries old. The flagged floor was covered with rush matting, such as Jan had seen in the markets; and down the middle of the vast room stretched a long table whose top was of many coloured marbles arranged in squares and circles. The dim light was filtered through tall, narrow windows of a greenish glass. Like living at the bottom of the sea, Jan decided, staring about her as she shifted from one foot to the other waiting for someone to come.

It seemed a long time. Were they busy inventing some story about Bianca not being there; or hiding the girl? Or had she made a mistake, and someone would presently appear to send her away because the Conte was too old, or too disinclined, to receive untidy girls with long blowing hair, and bare scratched feet in scruffy sandals? Perhaps they thought she was a stray tourist intruder.

Then suddenly Bianca Cellini walked in and stood a moment in silence, studying her visitor.

She was exactly as Jan had pictured her. At first sight, not unlike herself. But when one looked again, the Cellini girl was seen to be more delicate. A hot-house flower, Jan thought quickly, cherished and protected from every cold wind. She had the confidence of fine breeding and great wealth, a kind of sheen on her even though she was, at this moment, almost as untidy as her visitor.

Jan returned her curious stare with a quick feeling of dismay. This child would never survive in Paolo's world. She needed the sort of life her fiancé could give her, the rarified atmosphere which surrounded cherished women of fortune and position. Poor Bianca, poor Paolo! Marco was right, after all.

'You're the English girl,' Bianca announced. 'How did you know I was here? Did Francesca tell you?'

'No. I guessed. I tried to think myself into your mind, and I knew you must be on the island a long time before I knew where you were. How was it Marco didn't find you here?'

146

'He never asked.' Bianca laughed, a silvery peal full of gaiety. 'He wouldn't dare, in case my godfather discovered I was missing. He came, of course, to pay a formal visit; but I told my godfather I was in disgrace for some peccadillo and that it would be wiser for me to keep out of Marco's way that day. He is a gallant gentleman, old as he is, so he protected me and said not a word of my being here.'

'You don't feel ashamed of deceiving that old man?'

'Why should I? I've made him happy. He loves having me here. And I did visit Mamma, quite often, when Marco was away. So don't scold me, because you look about my age and I hardly ever meet anyone who is, except some of the island girls, and I can't talk to them. Your name is Jan, isn't it? Haven't you ever been in love, Jan?'

'I'm in love now. And it is not a happy love, Bianca, so don't give me that you-don't-know-what-it-feels-like routine, because I do know. I love a man I can never marry.'

'Poor you! But you are stronger than I am. You look stronger. You can look after yourself, can't you? I can't. I've been brought up to be fed, clothed, and taken care of by some man, the richer the better. I don't know any other kind of life. It isn't easy to be me, Jan.'

'It isn't easy to be anybody. We have to do the best we can. What's wrong with this man you're supposed to marry? Can you tell me? I'm sympathetic, really I am. I think an arranged marriage is dreadful.'

Bianca giggled. 'Tell my brother that!'

'I have. Several times.'

The Italian girl whistled, clear as a blackbird. 'And you're still alive! You're lucky not to be his sister. A great sense of family discipline, Marco has. It's because I was so young when our father was drowned, and he became a solemn, serious big brother, taking care of us all and of the business. Before that, he was so sweet. You can't imagine how sweet he can be, when he's not worried and anxious.'

'I've only known him worried and anxious. About you. Are you going to tell me about Rafaello? You can, you know.'

'Not here. Come up to my sitting-room. Would you like some wine or anything?'

'I'd like a drink, after the hot ride. I don't think I'm the right size and shape for a donkey. Could it be orange juice?'

Bianca's room was in a circular turret overlooking the sea. 'Like being in a ship,' she explained, 'because one cannot see any land at all. See? It juts out right over the water. I like it because the windows are bigger. There was no fear of attack from this side, you see, and they made larger spaces because this was the look-out for enemies.'

'Who were the enemies?'

'Saracens, I expect. Spaniards, Venetians, Normans, French, everybody was busy attacking everybody else all through the Middle Ages, and most of it happened around Italian shores. The Crusaders built this place, but whether they were coming or going I don't know. Why can't people live and let live?'

'Why, indeed? Rafaello?'

'Oh yes.' Bianca settled comfortably in the padded windowseat, with the orange juice she had collected on the way up. 'He's one of Them. The rulers, the fighters, the men who built *this*. Not those who put the stones one on top of the other, I mean the men who wanted to build it. Wouldn't you think there was something wrong with people who actually wanted to create a horrible place like this? You should see the dungeons!' She shuddered delicately.

'Does Rafaello have dungeons?'

'Not dungeons exactly. But he belongs to Them.

I can't talk to him. My mouth goes dry and I just can't find any words at all. Imagine living all one's life with a man one cannot talk to!'

'Does he talk to you?'

'He tells me things. But when I try, I always say something wrong. He corrects me, in front of other people. If I say a distance is three kilometers, he says very loudly, "Oh no, Bianca, you're wrong! It is three and a half kilometers." I wouldn't make anyone I loved look a fool, just for the sake of half a kilometer, would you?'

'No. Don't you think you might get used to him, in time? You would make a lovely Contessa.'

Bianca stared wistfully into her glass. 'I'd like a title. I'd like everything he can give me, except the man himself. It's sad.'

'Very sad. And you are also in love with another man?'

The girl's head shot up. She sat upright, spilling the juice, and stared at Jan. 'How did you know that?'

'First, because I guessed it. No girl would fight so strenuously against marrying a handsome, rich, and splendid fiancé if she didn't have some other man in mind. I gather you raised no objection to the betrothal in the first place?'

'I hadn't met Paolo then. And I didn't realise what a disastrous bore Rafaello was going to be. He's pompous.'

Drily, Jan said, 'I guessed he might be.'

'And secondly?' Bianca probed. 'What was the other thing?'

'I met Paolo. In fact, he kissed me.'

'*Paolo* did? The wretch! How dare he? Wait till I see him again!'

'It was an accident. He thought I was you.'

The lovely eyes widened. ' How could he make such

a mistake? He loves me.'

'It was momentary, I assure you. I was walking along your beach, looking down at a shell, and wearing your pink bikini. My hair was hidden. Yours is much lighter, and not as long. He came up out of the water like Neptune.'

'He swam round the headland, from his boat?'

Jan nodded. 'Expecting to see you there. So he pounced on a girl who looked like you, flung his arms round her and got kicked hard on the shins. But even without the kick he knew at once he'd made a mistake, and was very apologetic.'

'Ah, I see. He came behind you?'

'With his eyes full of sea-water. We sat on the sands a long time, talking—about you.'

'He adores me,' smiled Bianca.

'I know. He thinks you adore him.'

'But I do.' Bianca clasped her hands together earnestly, with an unconsciously dramatic gesture. 'If we can't be married I shall die. When I am with him, everything seems so right. And when I am with Raf, everything seems just a little wrong. As if someone had given the world a twist out of shape. Not much, but enough to spoil it.'

'Have you told your brother all this?'

'I've tried. But he has never been in love, so he doesn't know. When I am not with Paolo, I feel as if the soul has gone out of my body. Life doesn't go on. Time moves, but I am not living it. I'm just—waiting —for time to start again.'

'I know. I feel like that all the time.' Looking out of the high window, Jan saw a white boat, small as a toy, moving at snail's pace across the vivid blue. 'Like a boat which has lost its anchor. Adrift.'

Bianca hugged her knees and stared at Jan with wide eyes. 'You're in love—I can tell. When two people feel like that about each other, anything which keeps them apart must be wrong. I'm only staying away from Marco as a sort of demonstration, like the young people do on television. To make my point. But—' her head drooped forward, the curtains of her hair falling like wings on either side of her small, sad face, 'I haven't much hope of winning. All the big guns are against me.'

'But the biggest gun of all is for you—Paolo.'

'What can he do? Marco owns him.'

'Marco owns nobody, not even you. The world is wide, Bianca. There are other jobs. Paolo has brains and clever men will pay well for brains. If you want him, you must let him tell Marco he wants you.'

'He would never do that. I begged him not to. I was afraid for him.'

Jan covered the space between them, dropped on her knees and seized the slim shoulders in her strong hands. 'Bianca! Look at me! Tell me the truth. The honest truth, right from the depths of your heart. Do you really want to marry Paolo? I don't doubt you love him, but is it the sort of love which climbs mountains and crosses rivers? Would you mind not being really rich, the way you are now? Would you stand by him till he got on his feet again if Marco finished with him? Search your heart, Bianca. Are you playing with Paolo?'

'No, no, no, I am not playing. I mean it. Without Paolo, I believe I shall die. I'd rather be a nun for ever than marry Rafaello.'

Jan sat back on her heels. 'Very well. Get your things together and come home with me. This afternoon Paolo will come to the villa to ask your brother for you.'

'Marco will eat him. He doesn't know—'

'Don't you have any faith in Paolo? I have, and I've only met him once. I don't profess to love him, but I'm absolutely sure he'll do as he says. He will be fighting for the girl he loves. And you must be there, at his side.'

The tender mouth shook. 'You mean all this? It's true?'

'Every word.'

'Very well. I'll come. You'll—you'll stand by us, Jan? You're so much stronger than I am.'

'My dear child, it's no business of mine. I can't poke my nose into the affairs of the Cellini family. Try not to lose that fierce Cellini temper. Keep calm, and stick to what you want.'

'Paolo promised me he wouldn't. I wanted him to wait till I'd brought Marco round myself.'

'Paolo is a man, remember. And a man fights his own battles, if he's worth having.'

Bianca nodded. 'I'll come. If only Marco could understand what it is to be in love—'

'It would help,' Jan agreed wistfully. 'But stand firm and you may be able to make him understand. Even if he doesn't, at least he'll know you mean what you say. The time for these old castles is over, child. You and I belong to another century, whatever the men say.'

CHAPTER VIII

Jan, Pietro and the donkey went back alone. Bianca had promised to play chess with her godfather before lunch, and would not disappoint the old man. She would say goodbye to him, she said, and leave when he had settled to his siesta.

Going uphill on the donkey was worse than going down. After a while Jan tired of the struggle not to slide backwards over the creature's tail, and decided to walk. It was now very hot, the sun blazing on the exposed sections of the track, and the flies bothering Jan and the donkey. Pietro cared for nothing. He had his five hundred lire and jogged along on his hard little heels planning how to spend such a fortune. Jan knew she would have to pay his father for the hire of the animal, and hoped Pietro was wise enough to spend his tip before one or the other of his parents commandeered it.

The kitchen was in an uproar when the tired and dusty pair arrived; Maria-Teresa shouting at the top of her voice, and everyone else scuttled round at her orders, and adding to the commotion by a running commentary of his or her own. Jan was by this time accustomed to the colourful and passionate Italian way of carrying on a normal conversation, but this seemed more intense than the business of preparing the villa lunch warranted. So she asked, at the top of her voice, what was happening.

Maria-Teresa flung her arms above her head. '*Ma insomma! Siamo fritti!* We have guests for lunch. Here already! And these good-for-nothings lazing about and the Signore wanting to put the best before his guests, and—'

Jan was not alarmed, knowing that Maria-Teresa

produced a perfect meal every day for her employers, and that all vacant space was piled high with food in the course of preparation. 'Where is Francesca?'

'Dressing the Signora. And when you and the Signorina Bianca arrive, you are to go to your rooms by the side path, not through the garden or you will be seen. And to dress quickly in a good style for important people, please. *Santo cielo!* Where is *Sigorina* Bianca?'

'Coming after the siesta.'

'*Siamo fritti!*' The cook clutched the bosom of her apron in horror, then rushed to the stove where a pan spluttered.

Jan left the kitchen to its crisis and, only too anxious to avoid important guests in her present state, tiptoed lightly along the side path and stole into Bianca's bedroom without being seen. She showered quickly and dressed in the nicest dress she possessed, a trim pink linen. As she brushed her hair into its normal sleekness, she wondered whether she was supposed to join the family and their obviously important visitor, or whether she should tactfully take lunch in her room. If only Francesca would come, and explain what had happened to set the kitchen in an uproar and require the Signora to be specially dressed. Who was this guest?

She was doing her eyelashes when the maid slipped in. '*Signorina!* You are here, thank God and his angels! Did you find the Signorina Bianca?'

'I did. And she is coming home when her godfather settles to his siesta. I heard in the kitchen we have a guest for lunch. If it's someone terribly important, maybe I should eat here. Will you ask the Signora what I am to do, please? If you can, that is.'

'Too late. She is already with *him*. Oh, if only Bianca had returned with you, all would be well. The Signore is so angry and so polite. He is like Vesuvius

154

today, all fire deep down inside, and so pleasant on the outside. I pity him, I truly do. What will happen?'

'How can I say, until I know who the visitor is? Is it a business colleague, or one of the family, or what? Do stop wringing your hands and tell me.'

'Did they not tell you, in the kitchen? It is the Conte Alberghi.'

'Sounds impressive. And who is he?'

'Who is he?' Francesca's voice squeaked with astonishment. 'Does the Signorina not know? He is the betrothed of the Signorina Bianca.'

'*What!*' Jan's heart raced. The palms of her hands were damp. Rafaello here, at the villa? 'When did he come? Did he arrive without warning?'

'I think not. He found himself in Naples on business, and telephoned to say he would hire a motorboat and come out. That's what the Signore told Dino. Of course they went down to the harbour to meet him, and arrived back here ten minutes ago. The two *signori* are at this moment sitting on the *terrazzo* with cigars, and talking over their wine.'

'What has he been told about Signorina Bianca?'

The girl shrugged. 'I don't know.'

The aunt in Florence story, of course. With Bianca due to arive home within the next two hours, ready to do battle with her brother but completely unprepared to meet her fiancé. In spite of all that had happened, the girl was still engaged to the Conte.

'Francesca,' Jan said urgently, 'Bianca must not be allowed to walk into this without warning. Can we telephone the castle?'

'Not without the Signore hearing.'

She drummed her fingers on the marble top of the toilet table. 'Someone must go down. Not Pietro, he'll be tired out. He's only small. Is there anyone else who could take a letter?'

'Plenty. The kitchen is always full of empty minds and full stomachs. But we shall have to pay.'

Jan laughed shortly. 'That goes without saying! A thousand lire?'

The girl shrugged. 'It is hot now, and the messenger will lose a meal and miss the siesta.'

Jan hesitated. She was running short of Italian money unless she changed another travellers' cheque, which she was loth to do at this juncture. She had enough for her journey, but little over. 'Three thousand, then. I can spare no more.' It occurred to her that she could pay a good deal more and recoup it from Marco. His sister's arrival, in the nick of time, would suit him well, but unless she was warned that Rafaello was here, she would walk straight into disaster. And Paolo was due to arrive this afternoon. Would it be possible to intercept him, warn him to turn back? With these volatile, quick-tempered Italians, in such an inflammable situation, who could tell what might happen?

Francesca seemed to think the sum adequate. 'Write the letter. I will see that it is delivered.' Jan scribbled, in both Italian and English, praying that between her limited Italian and Bianca's schoolgirl English, the message would be clear enough. With the letter on its way, nothing more could be done.

So Jan, subduing the panic which threatened to swamp her, went out to the terrace and took her place discreetly behind her hostess. Marco greeted her with evident relief, plainly thankful for some distraction.

'Ah, our English guest! Jan, you at last meet my sister's fiancé. I have been telling him how kind you are, to say with Mamma during Bianca's visit to her aunts in Florence.'

The trouble about visiting so many picture galleries in Italy, Jan thought at once, is that one is always meeting the originals, in modern dress. Rafaello

Alberghi had the face of a typical Doge of old Venice; a proud head, eyes close together under high arched brows, a strong nose like a prow, a sensuous mouth. He bowed to her perfunctorily, as if assessing the English girl as unimportant. Then he spoke to Marco in a smooth, cold voice, full of quiet menace.

'Florence, my dear Marco? I have just returned from Florence, and naturally paid my respects to my future aunt-in-law. I assure you Bianca was not there. The aunts had not seen her for many months. Is it possible you don't know where she is, or with whom?'

There was a silence which quivered on the hot air. Marco's expression was tense. The Signora's hands were perfectly still. For a few endless minutes no one moved. Then Marco said: 'Ah, she had moved on, then, to her cousin's home in the country.'

Jan knew she must speak, but was unable to break the spell that held them all dumb. So it was Rafaello who shattered the silence, though his voice whispered like sprung steel.

'Does a young lady of your family come and go as she pleases, and with whom? My mother and sisters would not regard that as fitting conduct for a young girl, not yet of age, and unmarried. I shall require an explanation, please, and so will my mother.'

Marco came to his feet like a wrestler, his movement smooth and full of menace. '*Signore*, are you suggesting that my sister's conduct is less than honourable? If so—'

As the angry men faced each other, it was not difficult to picture the half-drawn swords of another century. In the split second before disaster, Jan's reflexes, trained to act in desperate emergencies, took over.

'*Signore*, there is a telephone message from the Signorina Bianca. Forgive me, I did not wish to interrupt your conversation with the Conte. She will be here soon after lunch, from her godfather's home. As you were engaged, I took the liberty of instructing Dino to meet her.'

Not a muscle of Marco's face moved. He must have had himself under rigid control from the minute the Conte set foot on the island. 'Thank you, Jan. I was just about to tell the Conte, Bianca intended to finish her tour with a visit to her godfather. Naturally, he was impatient for news of her.'

Rafaello, stiff and unrelaxed, smiled grimly. 'Naturally. No doubt she will tell me about her extensive tour when we meet. It seems she has travelled rather faster than you expected, *signore*?'

Marco shrugged. 'No doubt. I trust my sister, Rafaello. I assure you I do not have time to check on her movements from day to day. This aunt, or that cousin, or her godfather—she is impulsive and young, and visits like a butterfly visits the flowers.'

'The bloom of the butterfly is easily brushed off, *signore*.' Rafaello's inference was plain.

'By rough handling only,' Marco riposted.

His mother clapped her hands gently, a soft sound like the falling of leaves. 'Dear Bianca! How happy we shall be to have her home again, after her visits. She will have so much to tell us. Dear Raf, do sit down again and tell me all the news of your mamma. I long to see her again.'

Out of courtesy to his hostess, Rafaello Alberghi began a long conversation in Italian too rapid for Jan to follow. She realised, for the first time, that her own progress in the language had been largely due to the care Marco and the Signora had taken to speak slowly and clearly for her benefit. Even when Marco was scolding me, she thought with an inward smile, he took care I should understand every word.

Her mind was occupied with the problem of Paolo. If he failed in his promise and stayed away, it could only be because he was not man enough to face Marco and ask for Bianca; and that would be a tragedy for both of them. But if he arrived too early, before they had managed to get rid of the Conte Alberghi? She shivered with apprehension. As she worried about this, she felt eyes upon her, and looking up, met those of the Conte, studying her minutely. They were as cold and cruel as a serpent's. Their searching stare chilled her spine.

This was the Rafaello Bianca must have seen. This was what Marco could never see. The man was far from satisfied. Without a word, he made her understand that he thought her a liar. He would question poor Bianca mercilessly.

I cannot talk to him, she heard Bianca saying in her eyrie over the sea in the grim castle. No wonder! Those chiselled features, those unfathomable eyes, would silence any woman. For the moment, Raf was exercising his charm. But how would a wife fare, under his disapproval? There was no tenderness in that face. He would take a woman in arrogance, as of right. I'd as soon be married to a basilisk, Jan decided.

Luncheon was announced. Movement to the table eased the tension slightly. As Marco drew out Jan's chair, he bent forward and breathed into her ear, ' You'd better be right, whatever you've been up to! Heaven help you if you're wrong!'

She thanked Marco with a charming smile, but their eyes met and clashed. She was in for a bad quarter of an hour, when he was free to question her closely.

The Signora played the hostess delightfully, though Jan watched her anxiously lest a lapse should unwittingly betray her wandering mind. Such a lapse would undoubtedly be chalked up against the Cellini family and used to discipline Bianca in the future. Was Marco so blind that he couldn't see how terrible the young Conte must seem to a girl like Bianca? Young in years he might be, but centuries old compared with her fresh youth. Only this morning she had thought Marco right in choosing a man who could give his sister the cherished life of a rich *contessa*, and considered Bianca unsuited to the rough-and-tumble of marriage with an up-and-coming young executive. But far rather that, and the struggle for survival in a competitive world, than the cold torture of life with Rafaello Alberghi on his vast estates.

They had finished lunch, and lingered over coffee, to the point where the Signora and Jan were about to withdraw for the siesta, when Bianca arrived.

She was not alone. The casually dressed teenager of the morning had disappeared. Bianca looked superb in a simple white dress of impeccable cut, her hair piled high on her head which she held as proudly as a princess. Classically perfect as a figure on a cameo, she approached slowly, holding the arm of a tall old man with snow-white hair, the noble head and bold hooked nose of a classical Roman.

Jan's heart turned over. The men rose as the pair approached. This was a scene which could have happened any day amid the splendour of ancient Rome or the elegance of the fine city of Pompeii. The proud old man, the lovely girl, walking between the white columns and framed by the distant sea of lapis lazuli blue.

Jan thought, whatever is going to happen in the next few minutes, this is a picture I shall never forget as long as I live. It must be that Rafaello and Marco were equally struck by Bianca's entrance, for neither moved nor spoke, but waited for the pair to cross the marble terrace to the table as if under a spell.

Then the magic was broken. The Conte was presented to Bianca's godfather, Signor Bernini. He kissed his fiancée's hand. Bernini kissed the Signora's hand and then Marco remembered Jan standing discreetly at a slight distance. Everyone sat down and fresh coffee was ordered.

But Signor Bernini waved coffee away. 'I brought my goddaughter home,' he said severely, 'because she has something to say to the Conte Alberghi.'

'But naturally,' cried the Signora. 'He is her betrothed. They must discuss the wedding. Raf has been telling me how much his mother and sisters look forward to welcoming the child at his *palazzo*.'

Bianca cast a despairing glance at Jan, then looked down at her hands clenched tightly in her lap.

There was a silence. Rafaello looked at Bianca.

'Well, Bianca? You have something to tell me?'

She lifted her head and looked him steadily in the eye. 'It is between ourselves, *signore*. Not my mother or my brother—just you and me. As far as I remember, we have never spoken to each other alone until now. But if we may go indoors and be undisturbed for a while, I will tell you what I have to say. No, Marco, it is not your affair, but mine alone, so please let me say what I have to.'

She rose with dignity and laid her hand on the Conte Alberghi's proffered arm. Together, they disappeared into the house.

'Sit down, Marco,' said her godfather, in a voice which had to be obeyed. 'You too, my dear Signora, if you will have the grace to listen to me.

'First,' he said when they had re-seated themselves, 'I do not like that young man. Nor, which is more important, does Bianca. The child has been in my house for the last ten days and—'

Marco interrupted, 'Why did you not tell me, sir? I have been out of my mind with anxiety, trying to find her without creating a scandal. Surely I, as her proper guardian, should have been informed?'

Signor Bernini shot a glance under his bushy white eyebrows. 'And why? As her proper guardian, you engaged her to a man she detested, and would not listen when she tried to explain her feelings. If you have suffered, Marco my boy, I can only say it serves you right. You deserved it. Bianca saw to it that her mother saw her from time to time, especially after she received the Signorina Jan's message. She came for a few minutes almost every day.'

Marco buried his head in his hands. 'I am surrounded by traitors! Did everyone on the island know, except me? Jan, you too?'

'I guessed, Marco. But not till last night, after you —after we—well, late last night. This morning I went down and asked for Bianca, and there she was. I told her to come home.'

'Thank you for that, at least.' There was a touch of sarcasm in his tone. 'But your message? Who took that?'

She shrugged. 'No one. I just mentioned, here and there, that the Signora was fretting. Wrote it on a leaf, as you might say. Leaves flutter to the ground, in time.'

'Mamma?' He turned to his mother. 'Did you enjoy seeing me worry? My visits to the police, the private detectives I engaged? The visits I paid to our relatives, trying to find her without admitting she was missing? Was that amusing, when I am supposed to be at the head of a big business concern, earning the money to keep this place going? I came to the castle, *signore*.'

'You came. And had you shown the slightest concern for your sister's true happiness, I would have told you then.'

'Why am I accused?' He looked furiously from one to the other. 'I did my best for her. The Conte is young, handsome, charming, rich and of good family. Any girl, surely, could learn to love a man like that.'

'Never!' Jan said loudly, then clapped her hand

over her mouth. This was not her quarrel and she had no business to be present, even. She apologised at once, and said she would wait indoors until the discussion was over.

'You'll do nothing of the sort. You are involved in this. Sit down. Now tell me why you said Never! just now. You've only seen the man for an hour.'

'Half an hour is enough. I'd rather be kissed by a codfish! Marco, he's like one of those Pompeiian stone bodies, dead for centuries encased in molten rock. Only in his case, the living body is on the outside, the hardened rock is inside. For myself I'd rather die than marry such a man.'

'She agreed to the betrothal.'

Signor Bernini nodded his great head ponderously. 'She admits that. She was excited by the wedding of her friend last year, and the other bridesmaids were talking of their engagements. It was in the air, she said. And you presented the whole thing, Marco, in such glittering terms, and Alberghi, one must admit, is an imposing figure of a man. Oh yes, she agreed. It was not until afterwards she discovered she could not talk to him.'

'Is that all? That's shyness. A girl overcomes that when she is married. Shyness is natural to a young girl.'

Jan laughed shortly. 'Grow up, Marco.'

His eyes darkened. 'I seem to be doing so, very rapidly. I'm considered a successful man by a good many people. Those closest and dearest to me think that I am a complete failure as a brother and the head of my family. What is Bianca saying to the Conte in there?'

'She is breaking off the engagement.'

Marco's temper flashed. '*Ma insomma!* She has no right to do that. She should have left that to me. This is not just a boy and girl romance, it is a proper betrothal, and a lot is involved—the dowry, settlements, a certain amount of land, even business contracts. *Signore*, you are an experienced man of the world, you must have seen many such arrangements in your lifetime. I am sure your own marriage was arranged by your parents and your future wife's. You know this cannot be broken off simply by a girl's say-so. She should have consulted me first.'

'She did, but you wouldn't listen. You said it was nerves, and she'd get over it. So she naturally turned to her godfather. We gave you a little time to think matters over, and I agree with Bianca entirely, you are too stubborn and self-centred to think of this as anything but a business arrangement. Yes, I've seen arranged marriages and I've seen broken hearts. And now I'm old, I don't intend to go to my grave knowing my little Bianca is unhappy. I am rich enough to recompense you for any benefits you personally may lose, Marco.'

'If you were a younger man, I would take offence at that. I am not bartering my sister for benefits to come.'

'Stop shouting at each other!' The Signora spoke firmly, as if to children. 'No one has asked me what I think, and I am the girl's mother. I do not like the young man, so that seems to be four to one, Marco. You are in the minority, and after all, it is not you who will have to live with him for the rest of your life. And since we are speaking the truth for once, I detest his mother and his sisters. His mother was a cat when we were children together, and I am happy to say I once scratched her face. If my daughter is now engaged in scratching her son's face, I must say I am proud of her courage.'

They all stared. 'Mamma!' Marco gasped. 'Why didn't you say all that long ago?'

'I can't imagine! Perhaps because we were all
164

taught to be polite and say nice things about one another. Perhaps because our dear Jan brought a breath of fresh air into the garden and blew away some of the gossamer. Perhaps, my dear boy, because you make me cry sometimes.'

'I?'

'Yes, you. Bianca will be safe enough. She has a warm nature, she can love. She is so like her father. But you are too reserved, you keep yourself too strictly guarded. You have a heart, but no one has yet found the key to it. Once, before your father died, I thought you were different. I envied the woman you would love some day. Now I pity her, and you, because she may never find the key to open your heart to the sun and warmth, and happiness.'

Tears sprang to Jan's eyes. The gentle voice, so full of tenderness, was hurting Marco with its relentless baring of his mother's feelings. A muscle moved in his jaw and she ached to comfort him for the pain. Oh, my darling, my darling, all this is hurting you so much, and I have no shadow of right to help you. I, too, envy the woman you love, whoever she may be. She will have none of you, my dear, and I will have none of you because I want too much. I want your love as well as your name and money. If you could offer me that—!

Marco stood up, thrust his chair back. 'If I am hard it is because of the responsibilities I have had to carry. Don't forget that, Mamma, when you think I keep too strong a guard on my feelings. Outside these walls I live in a hard and ruthless world, where a man cannot afford to be soft. But don't imagine I don't know how to love, because I do. There is a girl who could have made a human being out of me again, as I used to be; but she will have nothing to do with me, and that is a hard fact I have had to accept, Mamma. If I show nothing, for God's sake don't get it into your head that I feel nothing. But all this didn't start with me, it started with Bianca. We are all concerned for her happiness, and if she doesn't want the Conte Alberghi, she doesn't. All I am trying to find out is why she didn't say so outright, instead of running away and creating all this trouble.'

The old man put a thin but still powerful arm round Marco's shoulder. 'We all make mistakes, my son. The fatal mistake is not to admit it.'

As if goaded beyond endurance, Marco turned on him. 'All right, I made a mistake—I admit it. It is not too late to put matters straight. Better now than on the wedding day—or after. But the blame is not entirely mine. It is partly yours, Mamma, for not telling me you disliked Raf and his family. Partly yours too, Signor Bernini, for not coming to me immediately my sister took refuge with you. I am a reasonable man, and—' He swung round to Jan and pointed an accusing finger. 'What you are grinning about?'

'Your description of yourself as a reasonable man. Of all the unreasonable creatures I've ever come across, you take the palm!'

'Unreasonable—!' Marco exploded.

But just then Rafaello and Bianca came out into the garden together, and they all turned to face the newcomers.

Rafaello was the first to speak. He drew himself up before Marco and Signora Cellini, clicked heels together and bowed stiffly. 'Bianco tells me she has changed her mind, and has asked me to release her from our engagement. I have told her most young women feel like this at some time during an engagement, and that she is suffering from a nervous crisis. However—' he stumbled, cleared his throat and went on, 'it appears her mind is made up. So I shall not hold her to the contract. I would have preferred some warning from you, *signore*, or from the Signora. But the girl has been honest enough to tell me, herself,

166

which I appreciate. Our family have no wish for an unwilling bride. Now, if you will forgive me, Signora Cellini, I will go. Thank you for an excellent lunch.' He kissed the Signora's extended hand formally, bowed again to Marco, and marched off, head erect, without another word to Bianca.

'He is a man,' Signor Bernini said quietly, 'and, I think, hard hit. Bianca, my dear child, that took courage. Was it difficult?'

The girl nodded. She was white-faced and trembling now the ordeal was over. 'I couldn't make him understand. He kept saying it was nerves. It never occurred to him that I didn't love him. And when that finally penetrated, he said it didn't matter.'

She sought her brother's gaze. 'Are you angry, Marco? I have been a great trouble to you.' She went to him, linked her arms round his neck and laid her cheek on his chest. 'I hated doing it, but I just couldn't make anybody understand. Only Jan understood, before she'd ever met me.'

Marco kissed her. 'I'm sorry, my pet. I was hard on you. Women have a wisdom of their own about men, I suppose. Raf seemed a decent sort of fellow to me. It appears I was wrong. Come, cheer up and forget it now.'

'Will he do something dreadful to you?'

Marco gave a crooked grin. 'I shouldn't be surprised. But these days men fight with business deals, not with cloak and dagger. So I daresay I shall be more than a match for Rafaello Alberghi, title or no title. Don't worry any more. Your godfather and your mamma have explained to me clearly that I am cruel, unnatural, selfish, and stupid, so—'

From the shelter of his arms, Bianca turned on the others. 'He is nothing of the sort. Marco would be the nicest creature in the world if only he knew what it was like to be in love. And one day, even that

167

miracle may happen. Then you'll see.'

Her mother held out her arms. 'Come, my sweet. Now all the trouble is over, it is time we all retired for the siesta. Marco, show my dear old friend to a room where he can rest, and later he will join us at tea. He dearly loves his English tea, I know.'

It was at this moment that Francesca, still in her pretty costume, appeared on the terrace and announced that the Signor Paolo Ricardo was at the gate and wished to speak with the Signore.

'Paolo!' shrieked Bianca, and flew across the garden towards the gate.

Marco scowled. 'The name is vaguely familiar. But why should he visit me here, and why should Bianca behave in that extraordinary way?' Suddenly he clapped his hand to his head. 'My lord! The villain of the piece!' He looked at Jan swiftly. 'You knew about this?'

'Since yesterday. I've been expecting him any time this last half-hour, which is why my knees have been knocking together. He's the man Bianca loves.'

'Is he indeed! How dare he come here!'

'He's in love, that's why. He may be scared stiff of you as his chief, but out of the office hours he's afraid of no one, where Bianca is concerned. So watch out, Marco. There are a pair of them and together they'll be more than a match for you.'

Marco smiled. 'Maybe. But I think I hold the winning card.'

'Don't you believe it! Paolo does. Look!'

Paolo and Bianca were coming across the garden hand in hand.

'Mamma—and Signor Bernini, this may be long and tiresome. If you would care to retire for the siesta?'

'Not a bit of it,' said Bernini, re-seating himself. 'I haven't had such an entertaining afternoon in years. It's better than a performance of any opera at La Scala.

I intend to sit through the next act.'

'So do I.' The Signora beckoned to Jan, who moved her chair into the shade of the palms and tucked a cushion cosily into the small of her back. 'And mind you play it well, my son. I like the look of this young man.'

CHAPTER IX

Bianca was radiant. Clasping Paolo Ricardo's hand, she presented him to her family, with an engaging pride and shyness.

'Marco already knows him, Mamma. He is a member of the staff, those Marco calls his bright young men. And this is my godfather, Paolo—Signor Orlando Bernini.'

In his clothes, Jan decided, Paolo looked less impressive. But it was a good suit, well chosen for the occasion. He seemed a young man marked for success in that indefinable but not-to-be-mistaken way one often saw in medical students. This was an ordeal indeed, for him, to encounter the Cellini family all at once. But he seemed equal to it, and his manner was an acceptable blend of modesty and confidence.

'Did I send for you?' Marco asked him distantly.

'No, sir. Nor did the Signorina. I came entirely uninvited, because I have something to say to you in private.'

'Very well, say it. In the circle of my family, I am in private. It is nothing my mother and our oldest friend cannot hear, I suppose?'

Jan shivered a little, feeling the chill of Marco's attitude. He will not give one inch. He will act the part of the heavy father because he feels it his duty, but please don't let him hurt these two too much. Bianca has taken as much as she can stand already, and happiness is so brittle a thing. *Please*, Marco, she wished ardently.

'Sir,' Paolo's voice was hoarse and he had to clear his throat, 'I wish to ask you for the honour of the Signorina Bianca's hand in marriage. We love each other, and she tells me she is now free of her former

170

engagement.'

Marco tilted his head and looked at the younger man through lowered lashes. 'A strange coincidence! What would you have done, if she had not been free? The Conte came here today by chance. You couldn't possibly have known. How is it, that as he leaves the stage, you enter?'

'I intended to come today, *signore*, because a man must do what he has to. As you say, it was a coincidence, and for me a fortunate one, that the Conte arrived today and Bianca was able to tell him she did not intend to marry him.' He smiled down at the girl beside him. 'That's all I know, sir—that she is free. My coming wasn't arranged.'

'And you want to marry my sister? What have you to offer her?'

'Nothing, *signore*, except my love and my future.'

Marco glanced down at his own powerful hands. 'Your future? That lies here, does it not? In my hands? Supposing you have no future?'

Bianca paled as the significance of the question reached her. But Paolo kept his eyes steadily on Marco.

'You have power, of course. But there are other companies in Europe who can use my brains and my training—'

'The training I gave you?'

'Yes, sir. I am grateful for it, and I think you should make use of it, not throw it away for others to pick up.'

'You don't think I should instantly dismiss you for impertinence?'

'That is for you to decide. I have made an honourable offer, but whatever you say, Bianca and I intend to marry. And where I go, she will go.'

Jan sighed suddenly. Marco was being hateful. He was deliberately goading Paolo.

'That sounds remarkably like blackmail,' Marco drawled.

'It wasn't so intended, *signore*. But you were trying to blackmail me, were you not?'

The tell-tale muscle moved in Marco's cheek. Jan, observing it, knew he was close to losing his temper. But when he spoke, his tone was as suave as ever.

'Don't be clever with me, boy. Bianca is not yet of age, and cannot marry without my consent. And don't imagine you will win that consent by threatening to leave the company and find employment elsewhere. I have friends—and my friends have friends.'

Bianca blazed with fury. 'That's not fair! Marco, you have no right to threaten like that! Mamma, tell him he cannot do it. Signor Bernini, dear sweet godfather, don't just sit listening to him. Tell him how wicked he is.'

Bernini patted her hand. He had been following the conversation shrewdly. 'Marco knows what he's doing, child. He needs no advice from me.'

The girl gave him a scathing look. 'You're as bad as Marco. I believed you were more human. Mamma?'

The Signora sat erect, her calm features betraying no emotion. 'Marco is so like your papa, dear child. Let him be.'

'But he's threatening Paolo. He mustn't do that. If we love each other, we can't help it. Paolo mustn't be punished by having his career spoilt, and doors shut in his face all over Europe. I'd rather give him up than have him suffer like that.'

Paolo put an arm around her shoulder. 'Don't worry. He can't do it to me. He can only threaten. He has rivals who would be only too glad to get hold of one of his hand-picked high-flyers. That's not my term for myself, *cara*—I'm not so conceited. But it's what men call us.'

'Never mind your future,' Marco interrupted.

'What about the present? Am I permitted to ask where you met my sister? Not under my roof, that I do know.'

'It *was* under your roof,' Bianca told him passionately. 'At the last dinner you held in Rome, for the group who had been to the Paris conference. Paolo was one of them. You said in your speech they'd all done brilliantly.'

Marco sat down, tilted back his chair and looked up at the couple who still stood side by side as though a powerful magnet held them together. As it does, Jan reminded herself. She was beginning to realise Marco was not getting all his own way in this encounter, and thought he knew it too.

'Oh yes,' he nodded two or three times, 'I am prepared to admit that the Signor Ricardo is a brilliant young man, with an eye to his future. He is ambitious, too. Quick to take advantage of his opportunities, I think.'

'Well then—' cried Bianca in triumph. 'You think well of him, so—'

Marco held up a restraining hand. 'Of his opportunities. Such as meeting the sister of the head of the Company. Young, impressionable, attractive, and *rich*. No, Bianca, let me finish. I admire a young man who can see so clearly that the quickest way to the top may not be by the sweat of his brow, but by hanging on to the skirts of a pretty girl who—'

'*Signore!*' Paolo sprang forward, bringing Marco to his feet. For a tense moment the men faced each other, not a pace between them. Paolo was breathing deeply, flushed with anger. Marco's eyes were bleak, so cold as to be cruel.

Bernini broke up the confrontation. 'Come, come,' he said easily. 'There are ladies here. Let us not quarrel. Signor Ricardo seems to have a good many qualities you admire, Marco, and our little Bianca is obviously very much in love—'

'I don't doubt it,' Marco agreed. He broke into irritability for a moment, and snapped, 'For heaven's sake sit down, both of you! You stand there like a pair of puppets. That's better. What was I saying? Oh yes, that I don't doubt Bianca's love for a moment. Anyone can see she's utterly infatuated.'

'Oh no,' breathed his mother softly. 'I think she truly loves him, dear. Don't be unkind to them, *caro*!'

'Thank you, Mamma,' whispered Bianca. 'I didn't know Marco could be so horrible. When Jan persuaded me to come home and talk to him—'

'I didn't know either,' Jan declared, 'or I'd never have suggested it. I thought he knew about justice. I thought he'd treat even an enemy with courtesy. I'm sorry, Bianca, I should have let you stay where you were, and play it your way.'

Marco swung round on his chair, and gave Jan a long, cryptic stare. 'So you are at the root of this, are you? I might have guessed. You knew all about this mysterious sweetheart, did you? Why didn't you tell me?'

Jan felt herself flush, the hot tide rushing up her throat and burning up to her forehead. 'I—I promised I wouldn't.'

'Promised who? Bianca?'

'Not Bianca—Paolo.'

'A guest in my house? And conspiring with a stranger against me? Keeping vital information from me, which you knew I needed? Indeed, for which I specifically asked you. You said—' his hand outstretched towards her, he snapped finger and thumb together. 'I remember—you said the secret was not yours to tell.'

She nodded miserably. He looked desperately unhappy, and the guilt of having deceived him, as in a way she had, weighed heavily on her.

'You have a strange sense of loyalty, *signorina*.' He returned to his examination of Paolo. 'So you paid attentions to my sister, did you? And no doubt met her elsewhere in Rome, without my knowledge?'

'Once, in the Farnese Gardens. To say goodbye, sir.'

Marco's brows rose in question. 'And all this love, all this passion and fury, comes from that one meeting —to say goodbye?'

'No, sir. We discovered we could not do it. I admit it was wrong, *signore*, to continue without your knowledge. Foolish, perhaps, not wrong. I came to the island many times, and we met on your private beach.'

'*Santa cielo!* On my very doorstep! You have the impudence of the devil, young man! You had no right to see her again.'

'He had every right,' Bianca cried passionately. 'Don't you *see*? Are you so blind, Marco? If you knew yourself what it is to love, you'd understand that when two people love each other as we do, anything —anything at all which keeps us apart, must be wrong.'

'I told you,' her brother said quite gently, 'that I don't doubt your love for him, sister *cara*! It is not beyond the power of any young Italian worth his salt to gain the love of an impressionable and inexperienced girl.'

'You're wrong! Rafaello Alberghi could not do it.' Jan spoke her thought aloud and could have kicked herself for doing so. Already in Marco's black books, she ought to have had more control. But Bianca flashed her a grateful glance.

'It is my love you doubt?' Paolo demanded stiffly. 'I have taken no advantage, *signore*. Love does not come by command. I should have loved Bianca at first sight whoever she was. If there is any way in which I can prove my love to your satisfaction—'

175

'You don't have to.' Bianca leaned across and pressed his hand fondly. 'I am the only person concerned, and I know you love me.'

Her brother relaxed enough to give her an affectionate smile. 'If you are so sure, *cara*, you won't mind his being asked to prove it?'

'I am not afraid.'

'Very well. Come to me in six months, Signor Ricardi, and ask me again. If you are both of the same mind then, I shall give my consent to the marriage.'

Bianca flung her arms round his neck and kissed him. 'You darling! I knew you would agree, when you had spoken to Paolo. Six months is a dreadfully long time, but we can wait. Thank you, oh, thank you!'

Marco held her away from him. 'Not so fast, Bianca! You must not see each other, or correspond, for the whole of that time.'

The girl pouted, but Paolo said, 'I agree. This is his test, Bianca. We can do it. I shall think of you every day and every night, and I shall work like a horse. Don't cry, my little love. The time will pass. You will be getting ready for your wedding, and I will find an apartment for us. We shall both be busy and happy.'

'One other thing,' Marco added. 'Bianca will have her dowry, of course. But understand there will be nothing else. You will get no benefit from marrying into the Cellini family, not a single *lira*. Now, or at any other time.'

'I am satisfied, *signore*. All I have asked from you is Bianca. I can look after her. Do I keep my job, or must I spend the six months looking for another?'

'Stay with the firm if you want to. It is your choice. That ends our interview. Say goodbye to Bianca. You will not see her, speak to her, or write to her for six months.'

' I may see him to the gate?'

Marco looked at his watch. ' You have ten minutes.'

When Paolo and Bianca had gone, Jan slipped away to her room. She guessed Bianca would return there, rather than join her family so soon. And she, Jan, felt she had had as much as she could stand of the Cellinis. Even that nice old Bernini had not been as helpful and sympathetic as he had at first appeared. He had actually nodded his great noble-looking head in pleased approval several times as Marco lashed out his cruel sentence.

Surely, too, Bianca's mother could have softened her son more than she had done? She hadn't even tried. Not a word of protest about that long separation; not even a protest against Bianca being cut off from all benefit in the family fortune after she was married.

Would Paolo come back to claim his bride? Bianca, of course, would not doubt him for a single moment during the six months.

What of Paolo? It was a long time to wait without a glimpse of the girl he loved. And what would Marco do to him, while he waited? Send him around Europe, on missions to Paris, London, Amsterdam? Anywhere where there were bright lights and beautiful women to be found, where life moved quickly and temptations fell into the way of good-looking men with Paolo's assurance and promise. Oh yes, without doubt Marco would make the test a fierce one. Pray God, for little Bianca's sake, he survived it.

The room, she realised now, was no longer hers. Its owner had returned. For her last night on the island, Jan would have to move. Luckily, most of her simple packing was already done. She had left out a clean dress for dinner, and the workmanlike navy and white spotted suit she intended to wear for the journey. Oh well, in the Villa Tramonti one did not worry. One rang the bell and gave orders. The thought amused her wryly. Like a private patient, without the trouble of having an operation!

Curiosity consumed her. What were the Cellinis talking about now? To stifle it, she took Bianca's guitar, curled herself into her favourite position on the chaise-longue, and played to herself softly, some of the plaintive, heartbreaking songs that were so popular among the youngest student nurses. The mood suited her own. *Good-bye, Marco. We shall never meet again. Good-bye to the Villa Tramonti, the azure Bay of Naples, the scent of orange blossom and lilies. To the whispering sea, the silver moon-path across the water, the vast canopy of stars. Good-bye, the Marco I thought I loved.*

I shall think of you often. Of your kisses, the presents you bought me, that horse-and-carriage drive across Rome, the lunch in the elegant restaurant-terrace of the Via Veneto. But I shan't cry for you, Marco, because I don't go on loving a man so hard-hearted, so iron-willed, so lacking in love. For a time, but not for ever. I shan't forget you asked me to marry you, but I shall, in time, be glad I refused.

When the sad little tune had finished, Jan looked up and saw Bianca leaning against the doorpost. Tears ran down her face, but she seemed unaware of them.

'You're unhappy too, Jan? Somehow I thought you were.' Bianca crossed the lovely white floor and flung herself down on her bed, flat on her back and staring up at the ceiling. 'Six months! This morning, before you came, it was for ever. So if Marco thinks six months is going to end our love, he's mistaken. We can wait.'

'You're not angry with Marco?'

'I could kill him—the horrible things he said to Paolo! I didn't mean I don't hate waiting, because I do. Every day will seem like a year. I meant Marco hasn't won. We shall play the waiting game, and we shall win in the end. I *have* won, already. I am free of Rafaello, and I can marry Paolo. We shall have Christmas in our own apartment.'

Jan plucked a few strings, making an ugly sound. 'You're lucky, then. For me, it is for ever, I think. I recovered from my first eternal love, quite suddenly. One day it was there, and the next—gone. How can that happen, I wonder?'

'Someone else comes along.' Bianca sat up suddenly, eyes wide with fear. 'You mean, someone else for Paolo? He travels, he meets people—they have lovely girls in those offices, you know. He meets them all the time. You don't think he'll fall out of love with me?'

'Trust him, Bianca. What's love, if you can't trust? My problem is, where am I to sleep tonight? I've been using your bed.'

Bianca wiped her tears away on a corner of the sheet. 'There's a guest room always ready. Francesca will move your things. Why are you packed, so soon?'

'I told you—tomorrow I go back to England. Already I feel sort of apart from all of you. I love your mamma, she's so sweet and gentle.'

'I know. She's mad, isn't she? I mean, all that about my father still being in the house, and forgetting everything one tells her. It's awfully weird to live with all the time. And what will Marco do about her, when I'm gone? I hadn't thought of that.'

'Marco thought of it.'

'He would. That man forgets nothing. He could get those nun friends of hers to come and live here, perhaps. But he'd hate having them around. They just sit there, with small smiles and their hands folded, and are so obviously terrified of him, he says. Or why don't you stay? She likes you, and you're good for her. She's been so much better since you came. Oh, please do, Jan.'

'That was Marco's solution, but it won't work. The Signora doesn't need a qualified nurse, only an understanding companion. All my training would be wasted, if I didn't use it to nurse people who are really ill. I explained all that to your brother.'

'But he would pay you far more than you could earn anywhere else.'

Jan sighed. How wealth-orientated these Cellinis were! 'Bianca, does it ever enter your head that there are things which are more important than money? Things which can't be bought?'

'It is entering my head that money is trouble. Trouble when you haven't any, and trouble when you have too much. And one can never be sure whether one's friends are truly friends and like you for yourself. I wish I knew more people like you, but I never get a chance to meet them. I will, when I'm married to Paolo. He and his friends belong to the real world, like you. And I shall belong, too, when I don't have the Cellini money round my neck like a millstone. Jan, what do you suppose Marco meant when he told Mamma there was a girl who could have made a human being out of him again, as he used to be? Is he in love?'

'I believe so. I think there is a woman he loves who won't marry him; and that he intends never to marry anybody else—that is, not for love. He might —he might ask a girl to marry him for convenience's sake, and if it suited him.'

Bianca shook her head violently, making the silken hair swing out. 'He would never do that. Never. Why should he? What sort of convenience?'

'Someone suitable, to look after his mother, for example?'

'He wouldn't be that crazy. He can afford the best

180

nurses in Italy, or, as you say, a suitable companion to live with her. No, if my brother says he's in love, he's in love. And he'll marry for that, or not at all.'

Jan's heart beat painfully. Why had she raised this subject, except for the eternal need of the lover to talk about the loved one, however much it hurt? Bianco had a naïve confidence in her brother, and it would be wrong to upset it by betraying him. Let her keep her romantic notions while she was so young and inexperienced. Time enough, in the future, for her to discover her brother to be a much more hard-headed and less idealistic character than she'd thought.

'One of us ought to go to the Signora,' she reminded Bianca. 'This has been a difficult day for her. She doesn't always sleep during her siesta, and likes someone to read to her. Will you go?'

The girl pulled herself up, with a groan. 'We can't unload our burdens on you any longer, can we? This six months is going to be deadly dull, but at least I have something to look forward to, now. Do you think me wicked, to hate this place so much? It's beautiful, but it can be a prison, Jan. Be thankful you're free, like the birds, to leave it when you want to go.'

Jan rang for Francesca, and supervised the moving of her things into a guest room. This was very different from the bright modern suite Bianca occupied. Cool, austere, furnished in dark woods exquisitely carved. The long curtains were of rose-coloured embossed velvet, the pelmets gathered together in swags supported by gilded cherubim. The four-poster bed had a heavy canopy, the headboard was carved in high relief with a scene of horsemen and chariots. The lamps were of wrought iron.

'You like it?' Francesca asked anxiously. 'It is only for one night. I wish you were not leaving us, *signorina*.'

'Thank you, Francesca. You've been kind and helpful, and I shan't forget you, or any of all this. The
Villa Tramonti will be often in my mind. Not that I
like this room particularly. It will be rather like sleeping in a church, don't you think?'

'It is old and they say all this is valuable. The
carvings are by a fifteenth-century artist—people come
to look at them. But you should see the Signore's
suite, that's truly beautiful. Not like this, old and
cold. He loves the light, and warm colours. It's a
pity I can't show it to you.'

'Perhaps I'll come again.' One says these things,
when one's heart is aching. They mean nothing. But
Jan wanted to be alone in this strange, silent room,
and examine her thoughts.

Suppose—just suppose—she had been wrong about
Marco?

Dinner was late because the Signora slept a long time
and Marco gave orders that she was not to be disturbed. Then it was too chilly to eat on the terrace.
A cool breeze blew off the sea, and with the sun gone,
an outdoor meal was uninviting. So, after all, Jan's
last dinner at the Villa was in the long formal dining
room, under the crystal-cut chandeliers and under the
eyes of the portraits lining the walls.

Marco was the perfect host tonight. With formal
charm, he took Jan on a conducted tour of the pictures.
'Not the best artists, but not bad. This was my grand-
mother. As you see, a beauty. In her day, Italy had a
king and a court. This is the dress she wore at the
wedding of one of the princesses.'

'Interesting,' Jan murmured politely. A chapter
was closing in her life. A short chapter, but full of
importance; one which might have changed her entire
future, had she been able to make any other decision
but the one she had made two nights ago. In time, all

this would fade into a past as remote as the world of the painted men and women on the walls. But there was the time between to be dreaded. The struggle for a personal peace, which could only be born within herself.

Until the talk with Bianca, she could have won through to that peace, given time. But now there was that tormenting, never-to-be-answered question—had she been wrong about Marco? What if she had been the woman he loved? What if, through lack of understanding, she had refused to marry him for the wrong reason?

She watched him discreetly during the long meal. He gave no sign. Never did he allow his eyes to meet hers. He seemed happy, released from the worries of Bianca's disappearance. With laughter, he described to his sister his efforts to find her; his exploratory visits to their relatives which had led him into so many evasive conversations.

Bianca, too, seemed happy to be reconciled to her family, and laughed aloud at Marco's descriptions. The Signora smiled from one to the other, serene now and remembering names and places as she could on her good days.

The waters will close over my head, Jan thought, and tomorrow evening it will be as if I had never entered the Villa Tramonti. For them—but not for me. I love him and I hate him—and I shall never know which is which.

After coffee, Marco disappeared as usual, to smoke a cigar on the terrace. Bianca sat by her mother, and presently embarked on a long monologue about Paolo's merits and charm. Jan listened lazily, her attention only half engaged, and was startled when Marco touched her shoulder. She had not heard him come in.

'Too cold outside for you tonight, but find a wrap

and come into my sitting-room. We need to talk about this preposterous journey of yours. We shall have to make an early start in the morning.'

Jan looked around Marco's own special sitting-room with interest and approval. This was how a man's room should look, an extension of his personality. She liked the deep white carpet, the comfortable leather chairs, the wall lined with books. There were several pieces of modern sculpture, and some modern paintings which were worth a closer look. It was a room for leisure, but for work too. Under a wide window she saw a vast desk covered in scarlet leather, and on it three telephones, black, white, and red. A stainless steel trolley carried suspended files in black leather, and on the wall there hung a large map of Europe, marked with red-topped pins.

'You're giving my room a critical look,' he smiled. 'Are you thinking it is much different from the rest of the villa?'

'I'm thinking it must be very like its owner.' I am printing it on my mind, she admitted to herself, so I can re-create it whenever I want. And I am a fool to do so. I should be planning to forget, not to remember.

He invited her to sit in one of the deep black leather chairs, and himself took a seat at his desk. 'The train times are ridiculous. You'll be travelling all night, with a Channel crossing to face in the morning.'

'That's right. It's cheaper that way. I don't waste money. Don't worry, I shall sleep in the train and I'm never seasick.'

'As you wish. That means you leave Rome at—' his fingers flicked over the timetables, then suddenly he pushed them all away. 'It won't do, Jan. You'll be travelling nearly forty hours. I hope you have first-class reservations.'

She smiled, with a touch of mischief. 'Second. I'm

a working girl, remember?'

'At least let me change your tickets. Or better still, let me fix you up with a flight from Rome direct to London.'

'Thank you, no.'

'Please, Jan. I owe you that much, for all you've done here.'

'All *I've* done? According to you, I have interfered, I've been disloyal, I've kept secrets I should not have kept. I borrowed your car without permission. One way and another, I've been a pretty fair nuisance. And let me remind you, you've already done a lot for me, apart from the original rescue. I will accept nothing more from you.'

'Tell me why?'

'Are you sure you mean that?'

'Yes. Suddenly I am poison to you. We were good friends, part of the time.'

'Very well. I won't accept another lira from you because I now know how you regard anyone who conceivably might be trying to cash in on the Cellini money. After listening to you this afternoon, giving that disgusting performance with poor Bianca and Paolo, I know what you think of people like me. That boy genuinely loves Bianca, he wants to marry her just as if she were an ordinary human being; and she loves him in the same way. But you—you've got to treat the whole affair as if it were one enormous confidence trick. And even when you finally agree to their marrying after six months' probation, you've got to make sure he never touches a penny of your hoarded gold; you're so determined on that, that you even plan to cut Bianca off from it. I don't happen to think money of your kind makes for happiness, but Bianca has never learnt to live without it, and it will go hard with her at first. But do you care? Oh, no, not Marco. Isn't there enough to go round, that you're so eager to cut her off?'

Her anger had swelled as she gave voice to all the unhappiness of the afternoon, till she ended what started as a simple statement as a tirade. Lord, I sound like a fishwife, she thought with shame, but it had to be said.

He was staring at her in amazement. 'Is that what you think of me? A miser, a grasping animal, not caring how I hurt others in my greed for money?'

'I didn't, until I heard you this afternoon.' Suddenly her anger collapsed. She said hopelessly, 'What else could I think?'

'You could perhaps have decided that girls like Bianca, who have lived a sheltered life, need some sort of protection. Look,' he swept his arm across the wide desk, 'tomorrow morning, every detail about that young man will be on this desk—his home, family, prospects, character, everything. Yes, even his love life, if he has one. We are nothing if not thorough in our business. He has been selected for special attention, special promotion. He has brains and ability. But *what else*, Jan? Marrying the boss's sister can be a good route to the top for an ambitious man. I had to make sure of his true intentions.'

She gripped the arms of her chair. 'You mean, it's nothing more than a test? No more than that? You didn't mean that part about cutting her off from the family?'

'Could I do that to my sister? If Paolo still wants Bianca in six months' time, they will marry with my blessing and he will become part of the family. As her husband, he will take his proper place in the management as soon as he can take the responsibility. If I'm satisfied with the reports I get, his promotion will start at once. Don't you see, I dare not risk a girl like Bianca being exploited by a fortune-hunter? Once I'm satisfied, she'll have no grumble about my treatment of my brother-in-law.'

'I'm sorry. I didn't understand. You are a difficult and devious person, Marco. One could never come to the end of trying to know you.'

He said, with a pretence at petulance, 'Bernini understood. So did Mamma.'

'Ah yes, I saw they approved. I see now why they did. They have lived in your world and know about its ways. I thought it was because everything Marco does is perfect in their eyes.'

He laughed at that. 'What? After you'd heard the pair of them scolding me for the fiasco of the Alberghi affair?'

'That was embarrassing for me. I shouldn't have been there. They shouldn't have done it, in the presence of a stranger.'

There was a silence. She heard him sigh lightly. Then, pulling up a chair to face hers, he took her hands between his.

'Jan, look at me. Two days ago I asked you to marry me. Do you remember?'

'One doesn't forget a thing like that. I shall always remember.'

'Unhappily for me, you preferred your career. You made that very clear. But I want you to know that a man never regards the woman he loves as a stranger.'

Jan began to tremble. She tried to speak, but words would not come. Time ceased. Slowly, she raised her eyes to meet his.

'Love?' Her voice quivered. 'You didn't speak of love.'

'Does a man invite a woman to become his wife, unless he loves her? I thought in your country you believed in marrying for love. I thought you would understand.'

Tears trembled on her lashes. 'Oh, Marco, I was such a fool. I thought you'd never be able to marry such an ordinary girl, from an ordinary sort of family. No dowry or anything like that. I thought you couldn't possibly want me for a real wife.'

'Then why on earth did you suppose I asked you? Jan, there's something behind all this. You're an intelligent girl. So how could you believe I didn't mean exactly what I said?'

'It was the Alberghi affair. You were so downright about who married whom, and the joining of great estates and fortunes, and properly arranged marriages —it was all new to me. How was I to know nothing of that applied to you? I imagined you'd be looking for a girl with a title, or vast fortunes; a father-in-law with a great commercial empire. I never saw myself in that context at all.'

'So?' His dark eyes questioned her.

'I thought you wanted someone to look after your mother, mostly.'

'But I spoke of a family—children. At least I think I did.'

'I know.' She was crying openly now. 'That's what made it so awful!'

He took out a fine linen handkerchief and blotted away the tears tenderly. 'Another thing I'm not good at —proposing marriage to the girl I love. I seem to have made a pretty grim mess of it, don't I?'

She gave a shuddering sigh, and blinked away the last of the tears. 'You never said about loving me. That was the trouble. You said you were rich, and could give me things. And money doesn't count at all—not with loving. I'm sorry, I didn't mean to cry. I feel so terrible about not understanding everything about you. I kept hating you, and loving you at the same time, and being so mixed up.'

'Loving me? You did say that? Is there some hope for me, then? Come, *cara*, please stop crying. It's my fault. Let us wipe out the last two days and start all

188

over again. Let's begin where I fell in love with you.'

' I can't believe you ever did. Mostly you were scolding me.'

' I? What nonsense! Do you know you're the only woman in my whole life who ever dared disagree with me, and tell me I was wrong? Do I remember complaining to you that all the girls I knew were exactly the same little dears, turned out by the dozen in the same pattern?'

' I remember your saying so. Do you mean nobody ever told you you were talking rubbish, or that you'd made a mistake?'

' No *woman*. Except Mamma, and she said it dotingly, so I never took any notice. And lately, of course, Bianca, spurred on by this love of hers. Love gives one terrible courage, have you noticed?'

' Where you first fell in love?' she reminded him.

' Ah, yes. I saw you swinging up the Spanish Steps, and a sort of delight twisted inside me, and set me on that breakneck race down the steps.'

' You said that was because you thought I was Bianca.'

' Well, I had to think of something. Besides, I did, just for a minute. As soon as I discovered you were not Bianca, the delight started again. I was so pleased you weren't.'

She lifted his hand, laid it to her cheek. ' I don't believe you for a moment! You are inventing all this, but go on. That you take the trouble to invent it shows me you love me.'

' Hope rises in me. Is it possible you love me?'

' I love you. I can't remember when it began, but it seems to have been going on for a long time. Actually, it's such a short time. Is it enough?'

He swept that aside. ' Enough for us. We have all the rest of our lives to learn to know each other. I shall find out six new things about you every day. If

I ask you again, will you marry me, my heart's love?'

'Oh, Marco, for two whole days I've been terrified I wouldn't get a second chance.'

He gathered her into his arms, rocking her gently as if he would never let her go. 'You won't hold against me my family, my fortune, my terrible importance and my wicked cruelty to my poor little sister?'

'I promise I won't. I'll be happy as long as you give me the one thing that matters—yourself.'

'That I have already done.' He kissed her now, a long, deep kiss, so different from that other, earlier kiss. A kiss born now of returned love, trust given and giving; of tenderness and joy.

The moon sent a questing beam across the white carpet, and to the foot of the wide desk. 'It's late,' he said reluctantly, 'and Mamma must be weary of listening to the perfections of one Paolo. So let us go and tell her about us.'

His arm round her waist, her head on his shoulder, they crossed the terrace, where the scent of lilies hung on the night air. How difficult this man was to understand, Jan thought, her heart alight with .pure happiness. But how well worth understanding after all.

The masquerade was over. This was real at last.

the universal language

That's why women
all over the world
reach for

Harlequin Romances

...from the publisher that
understands the way you feel
about love.

Let world-famous authors thrill you
with the joy of love! Be swept to
exotic, faraway places! Delight in
romantic adventure!

Harlequin Romances
Six brand-new novels every month!

Available at your favorite store or through
Harlequin Reader Service

In the U.S.A.
1440 South Priest Dr.
Tempe
AZ 85281

In Canada
649 Ontario Street
Stratford, Ontario
N5A 6W2

FREE Harlequin romance catalogue

A complete listing of all the titles currently available.

Harlequin Reader Service

IN THE U.S.A.
1440 South Priest Dr., Tempe, AZ 85281

IN CANADA
649 Ontario St., Stratford, Ontario N5A 6W2

Please send me my FREE Harlequin
Reader Service Catalogue.

Name

Address

City

State/Prov.   Zip/Postal